The Babysitter Chronicles is published by
Stone Arch Books,
A Capstone Imprint
1710 Roe Crest Drive,
North Mankato, Minnesota 56003
www.mycapstone.com

Library of Congress Cataloging-in-Publication Data
Green, D. L. (Debra L.), author.
  Kaitlyn and the competition / by D.L. Green.
    pages cm. — (The babysitter chronicles)
  Summary: Thirteen-year-old Kaitlyn Perez is a very professional and well organized
babysitter, but suddenly she finds herself in competition with a boy and the only thing
she knows about him is that his nickname is Doc, he lets the kids he is babysitting run
wild, and he is probably in her class—and that is only the beginning, as the stress causes
her to quarrel with both her best friend, Piper, and her sister, Eve.
  ISBN 978-1-4965-2754-7 (library binding)
  ISBN 978-1-4914-8861-4 (paperback)
  ISBN 978-1-4965-2758-5 (ebook pdf)
1. Babysitting—Juvenile fiction. 2. Money-making projects for children—Juvenile fiction.
3. Best friends—Juvenile fiction. 4. Schools—Juvenile fiction. 5. Sisters—Juvenile fiction.
6. Hispanic American families—Juvenile fiction. [1. Babysitters—Fiction. 2. Moneymaking
projects—Fiction. 3. Best friends—Fiction. 4. Friendship—Fiction. 5. Schools—Fiction. 6.
Sisters—Fiction. 7. Hispanic Americans—Fiction. 8. Family life—Fiction.] I. Title.
  PZ7.G81926Kai 2016
  813.6—dc23
  [Fic]   2015032133

Designer: Veronica Scott
Cover illustration: Tuesday Mourning
Image credits: Shutterstock: Guz Anna, design element, Marlenes, design element,
Woodhouse, design element, Vector pro, design element; Ron Wohl, pg. 150

Printed in Canada
102015   009223FRS16v

The BABYSITTER Chronicles

Kaitlyn and the Competition

by D. L. Green

STONE ARCH BOOKS
a capstone imprint

Sitter Smarts

Babysitters should prepare
appealing activities for children.

$$Chapter\ 1$$

I couldn't help giggling at the giant sunflower—AKA my older sister, Eve—as she walked into my bedroom.

"Ha-ha. Real funny, Kaitlyn," my sister said with a scowl. "These petals around my head weigh a ton. I need a warm bath, twelve hours of sleep, and a long vacation."

I stared at the yellow felt petals around Eve's face and the bright green leotard covering her arms and legs. "Looking at you sure makes me appreciate babysitting. It's a much better job than working at children's birthday parties," I said.

"Any job is better than working at children's birthday parties. You don't even want to know how I lost some of my petals. It involved rowdy six-year-olds with very poor scissor etiquette." Eve threw her petal headpiece onto my rug and walked toward my bed.

I blocked her path. "Please don't sit on my new comforter."

"I won't stain it, Kaitlyn," Eve said.

"Last week, you came home with chocolate all over your penguin costume. The week before, you had clumps of dirt in your duck feathers. I just don't want anything tarnishing my new comforter," I said. "No offense."

"Offense taken," Eve said. But fortunately she changed course without saying another word and sat on my old wooden desk chair.

I pointed at a bright pink splotch on her bright green tights. "What is that on the knee of your tights? Bubble gum? Cotton candy? Vomit medicine?"

Eve sighed. "I'm too tired to care. I hate my job."

I didn't blame her. Her job was pretty terrible. She worked as a face-painter at children's parties. She was paid minimum wage and had to wear awful costumes.

"There was one good thing about the party today, besides earning money," Eve said. "The guy who made balloon animals there was *sooo* cute. We snuck off for a few minutes to eat pizza in peace and exchange phone numbers."

I wrinkled my nose. "You snuck off during the middle of the party? To flirt with a guy and eat your client's pizza?"

"Sheesh, Kaitlyn. You make it sound like we ran off with the birthday girl's presents," Eve said.

"It just seems unprofessional. Like Mom says, '*Si vale la pena hacerlo, vale la pena hacerlo bien.*'" That was Spanish for, "If something's worth doing, it's worth doing well."

"Oh, lighten up," Eve said. "You know, you'd be happier if you chilled out a little."

I crossed my arms. "I'm not taking advice from a giant, tattered sunflower with pink mystery gunk on her knee."

"Fine. You won't feel so superior tonight when I'm at the hottest party in school and you're in your room reorganizing your closet or whatever."

"I'm going out tonight," I said.

"Where?" Eve asked.

"I'm babysitting."

Eve snorted.

I glared at her. "Save your snorts for the next time you have to wear a pig costume. Babysitting is a lot better than dressing up as a dorky flower and painting the faces of kids who cut off your petals and smear strange stuff on your stem."

"Whatever. See ya." Eve left my room.

I called out, "Wouldn't want to be ya!"

But I sort of did want to be her.

Obviously, I didn't want Eve's horrible job. And even if I had her job, I would never take an unauthorized, unprofessional break to eat pizza and trade phone numbers and flirt with a cute boy.

But I would "want to be ya" if it meant getting invited to the hottest parties at my school. Or even the not-so-hot parties. I wouldn't mind a warm party or even a lukewarm one.

Eve was three years older than me. But it wasn't our age difference that made Eve the life of the party and me . . . well . . . not even at the party. When Eve was thirteen like me, she'd gone to a bunch of bar and bat mitzvah parties, even though we weren't Jewish. At fifteen, she'd been invited to a ton of Quinceañera parties and had a zillion friends at her own Quinceañera party. And this year, she'd spent many nights at Sweet Sixteen parties. I, by contrast, hadn't been to a party in months.

The difference in our popularity couldn't be blamed on our appearances either. Everyone said we looked alike. We both had wavy brown hair and dark eyes and heart-shaped faces.

Simply put, I was a shorter, less-curvy version of my sister.

It was our personalities that made us so different. I'd always been careful. Eve had always been careless. I didn't want to leave the house with a wrinkle in my clothes or a hair out of place. Eve didn't even notice stray wrinkles or stray hairs. I played everything by the book. Eve just played.

I wanted to play too, to get invited to cool parties, to goof off with cute boys, to totally relax and have fun. I enjoyed babysitting every Saturday night, but it didn't make up for my sad social life.

I stroked my comforter, which always cheered me up. Made of pretty lilac silk and embroidered with sweet ivory birds, my comforter was soft and beautiful. My parents had refused to pay for it, claiming it was overpriced and would get stained easily. They refused to pay for a lot of things. My mother worked with children in foster care. My father managed a food bank. In their spare time, they volunteered at a homeless shelter. Compared with the kids they saw every day, Eve and I had more than enough possessions. But Eve and I didn't see it that way. So I had bought my comforter with the money I'd earned babysitting. I cherished it. It wasn't the same as an invitation to a hot party. It wasn't even the next best thing to it. But it was mine.

I took my babysitting bag out of my closet and made sure I had everything I needed for tonight. Two educational board games: Check. Six library books to read to the children: Check. Rubber gloves for light housework after the children went to bed: Check. Checklist for the parents, specifying what the children did in their absence: Check.

I grabbed the bag and my cell phone—which hadn't cost much, but came with a pricey two-year service contract—and went outside to wait for my client.

Mrs. Sweet pulled up a few minutes later. "Good to see you, Kaitlyn," she said as I climbed into her minivan.

"You too." I smiled at her. "And I can't wait to see Mikey and Lucy. It's something I look forward to all week."

Mrs. Sweet didn't respond. That was a bit strange. She was usually pretty chatty.

After a few minutes, I said, "I'm sorry I couldn't babysit Wednesday night. I had a big algebra test the next day."

"We should have given you more notice," Mrs. Sweet said. "But no worries. We found another sitter."

"I hoped she worked out all right," I said. But I was sure she hadn't worked out as well as I did. Mrs. Sweet had said I was the best babysitter her children ever had. My former client, Mrs. Hernandez, had said the same thing. Unfortunately, the Hernandez family had moved away last month.

"He," Mrs. Sweet said as she pulled into her driveway.

"He?" I asked.

"Yes. He—our babysitter—worked out just fine."

"Oh. Well . . . great." I hoped he hadn't worked out too fine.

When we got inside, Lucy barreled into me and gave me a hug. I hugged her back. She was five, the perfect age for babysitting. At that age, most children had left the tantrum and diaper stage but were still very cute. Lucy was adorable, with big brown eyes and curly black hair on a tiny body. I had the best job in the universe.

I hugged Mikey next. He was very cute too, with a short, stocky body like a miniature foot-ball player. He squirmed away after a few seconds. Like most seven-year-old boys, he didn't like to stay still.

I bet Mikey and Lucy hadn't hugged the other babysitter the way they hugged me. He might have been "just fine," but I was the best sitter they ever had.

Mr. and Mrs. Sweet reminded me about the children's bedtimes, informed me when they'd return, kissed Lucy and Mikey goodbye, and told them to be good.

"They're always good," I said. That wasn't exactly true, but parents didn't want to hear about their children's faults. Besides, on the whole, Lucy and Mikey were good kids.

After the Sweets left, I sat on the couch with my babysitting bag and said, "I got some new books from the library to read to you. We can start with those, or we can play a board game."

Mikey and Lucy stared at me in an odd silence, as if they'd forgotten the English language.

I pulled a couple of books from my bag. "This one's a cool rhyming book. And wait till you see the fun pictures in this one."

Usually they sat close to me as I took out books, squealing sometimes when they saw old favorites or bright new ones. But tonight they stood a few feet away. Lucy stared at me solemnly. Mikey actually frowned.

"Is something wrong?" I asked.

"Can we play tag?" Mikey asked.

I shook my head. "Sorry. It's too dark outside."

"We can play tag in the house," Mikey said.

Lucy ran to Mikey, pushed him, and said, "Tag! You're it."

Mikey ran to me and shoved me. "You're it, Kaitlyn!"

"Don't do that," I said.

"I was tagging you," he said.

"No tag in the house."

"But Doc played tag with us in the house," Lucy said.

"Doc?" I asked.

"Our other sitter," Mikey said.

My jaw clenched a little.

"Yeah. He was fun," Lucy said.

My jaw clenched a lot.

"He told us funny jokes too," Mikey said. "Knock-knock."

"Who's there?" I asked, hoping they'd forget about playing tag and *really* hoping they'd forget about Doc.

"Smell mop," Mikey said.

"Smell mop who?" I said.

Mikey and Lucy started cracking up, as if they'd just heard the funniest joke in the history of jokes. I didn't get it, but I smiled to humor them.

"Smell my poo!" Mikey shrieked. "Get it? You thought you were saying 'Smell mop who,' but I made you say 'Smell my poo!'"

"Smell my poo! Smell my poo!" Lucy yelled.

I dropped the smile. "That joke isn't nice."

"Doc thought it was really funny," Mikey said.

I didn't know who this Doc character was, but I didn't like him. Not at all.

The kids started running around the room, flailing their arms and yelling, "Kaitlyn said to smell her poo! Smell her poo! Smell her poo!"

"Okay, guys," I said, trying to keep my voice even. "How about a nice game now?"

"Tag!" Mikey said.

Oh, no. Not that again.

Lucy tagged Mikey hard on his chest and ran off.

He chased her around the living room. They almost hit the glass cabinet.

"Stop! No running in the house," I said.

It took a few minutes, a few more commands, and finally a few pleas to get the kids to stop running. But they finally did.

"You're no fun," Mikey said, crossing his arms.

"Yeah." Lucy crossed her arms. "Doc is ten hundredity times funner than you."

I sighed. Then I made my voice as perky as I could—ten hundredity times perkier than I felt—and said, "I brought over that game you liked a few weeks ago, the one where you have to turn over a cool card and find its match. Let's play!"

"All right," Mikey grumbled as if I'd just suggested they do homework.

"All right," Lucy grumbled like her big brother.

We sat at the kitchen table and played the game. Mikey said it was way less fun than tag. Lucy kept trying to get me to say "Smell my poo" again. But at least they weren't running around the house anymore.

After the game, I made the children brush their teeth, read them a few of the books I'd brought, and put them to bed. Their laughing fit and game of tag must have tired them out. They went to sleep easily.

Then I tidied the house and filled out my parental checklist. I wrote about the game we'd played, noting that it helped strengthen the children's memories and logic skills. I also wrote that the children had been quite spirited, a nicer way of saying wild and exhausting.

I was doing my math homework when Mr. and Mrs. Sweet came home. After I planted on a smile and said that everything had gone great, they paid me. Yahoo! Now that I'd bought a cell phone and a comforter, I was saving money for my monthly phone bill and nice clothes. My parents' idea of shopping meant combing the sales racks at discount stores. No thanks. I wasn't a total fashionista, but I tried to avoid out-of-style clothes in ultra cheap material and weird colors.

I was too tired from Mikey and Lucy's antics to make much small talk on the way home. Mrs. Sweet was quiet too. As we approached my house, I said, "Thank you for the ride. I'll see you next Saturday at the usual time."

Mrs. Sweet cleared her throat and said, "Actually, no."

"You and Mr. Sweet aren't going on your weekly date night?" I asked.

"We really appreciate your efforts, Kaitlyn." After a long pause, she finally said, "We've decided to use Doc from now on."

"Doc?" My voice squeaked.

"Yes. The other babysitter."

The guy who laughed at awful potty jokes and encouraged Mikey and Lucy to run inside the house? The Sweets were ditching their best-ever babysitter, who'd been at their house every Saturday night for six months, in favor of someone who'd only spent a few hours there last week?

The guy was named after one of the seven dwarves! If he didn't work out, would they hire Grumpy and Sneezy?

"I hope there are no hard feelings, Kaitlyn."

Of course there were. Hard as a rock. As a boulder, really. Feelings as hard as a giant boulder reinforced with steel and coated with diamonds. But I was a professional, not a goofy amateur like Doc. So I took a deep breath and croaked out, "No hard feelings."

Then I opened the car door and croaked, "Okay. Um. Thanks," which did not sound at all professional. I hurried from the car, grabbing my babysitting bag on the way out. It banged hard against my leg, leaving me with a dark, angry bruise.

Sitter Smarts

Babysitters should promote
their services.

Chapter 2

I spent all day Sunday organizing the kitchen. I sorted the junk drawer, matched bowls to their lids, and alphabetized the spice rack. I wished there were more to do in my house, but I'd already cleaned out the garage last month after a tough history test, organized the linen closet after I got a humongous zit on picture day, and put our family photos in albums after a boy at school called me Stork-Legs. Though my stress-organizing improved our house, it didn't actually make me feel better. I still felt miserable about losing my babysitting job.

On Sunday night I tried to brainstorm, jotting down every idea that crossed my mind. (My first idea was to figure out who Doc was and have him killed.) Then I read through what I'd written and crossed out anything that wouldn't work. I ended up with a grand total of one good idea: Find other people to babysit for. Easier said than done.

My rotten mood hadn't lifted by Monday. But Mondays, in general, are better at crushing moods than improving them.

My best friend, Piper Young, was grumpy too. We sat across from each other at the school lunch table and exchanged lunches, as usual. My parents always packed me leftovers from dinner. Boring. Piper always packed a sandwich, fruit, and something junky, which she found boring. Today it was crunchy peanut butter and cherry jam on sourdough bread, fruit cocktail, and a Twinkie. Yum.

"Be kind to me. I'm in mourning," Piper said with a catch in her throat. "Princess died."

"Oh, no," I said. I tried to remember who Princess was.

Piper sighed. "My poor, sweet, loyal goldfish."

Oh. Her goldfish. Piper's pets meant so much to her. The loss of any of them, however small, was devastating to her.

I reached across the table, patted Piper's arm, and said, "I'm sorry. Princess was such a special fish." That last part took some acting skills. I really was sorry that my best friend was upset, but I didn't actually think Princess was that special. Piper said each of her goldfish had its own unique personality, but it seemed to me they all just swam around and nibbled food.

Piper told me about finding Princess Saturday night floating upside-down in the aquarium, fishing out her plump, gold body with a net, and burying her in the backyard on Sunday.

I was glad that Piper had other pets to comfort her in her time of need: namely, a dog and cat that I adored; two other goldfish; two chickens; and a hedgehog, all of which I tolerated; and a snake and a bearded dragon lizard, which I avoided.

Piper stared down at my unopened lunch bag and said, "I buried Princess next to Fred, my departed hermit crab, and Chester."

"Ah, Chester. Your beloved pet rat," I said to show Piper I remembered him. I tried not to make a face.

"The funeral was nice. I sang, recited a poem, and buried Princess with a bit of fish food."

"Princess was lucky to have you as her owner. And now she's filling Heaven with pretty little bubbles," I said.

Piper nodded, and I ate a large chunk of the Twinkie.

"How was your weekend?" Piper asked.

"Not good." I told her about losing my babysitting job to Jerkface Doc.

"I'm sorry," Piper said in a sympathetic tone that probably took some acting skills on her part too. Piper liked children about as much as I liked snakes. When we watched *The Sound of Music*, she supported shipping the kids off to boarding school. She said that children should be neither seen nor heard. She wanted babies banned from airplanes, restaurants, movie theaters, and malls. But she didn't mention any of those things today. "What will you do for money now?" Piper asked me.

"I'll try to get another babysitting job."

She frowned. "Haven't you suffered enough?"

"I like little kids," I said.

"Me too," Piper said. "I like them cooked medium-well and lightly salted."

We laughed, something I hadn't done since getting fired on Saturday night.

Piper finally opened my lunch bag. She took out the leftover tuna empanadas and frowned. "I can't eat these after just burying Princess."

"Sorry. If I had known you'd just lost your goldfish, I would have brought a leftover chili relleno instead. Do you want your sandwich back?"

She shook her head and pulled out the churro I'd packed.

"I'm going to knock on all my neighbors' doors this weekend and offer my babysitting services," I said.

"You should also give out flyers with your name and number on them," Piper said.

"Good idea."

"Here's another idea," Piper said. "Find out who this Doc guy is and have him killed."

I smiled at her. "I thought of that already. Great minds think alike."

She smiled back. "And apparently so do mediocre minds."

We laughed again.

"Let's work on the flyer during English class. I need to keep busy in there," Piper said.

"How about paying attention to the teacher and taking notes to help you learn?"

Piper made a face. "*Ugh*. No. Why would I want to do that?" We laughed again.

"Once you get a new babysitting job, maybe you should do what Doc did," Piper said.

"Steal jobs from other babysitters?" I asked.

"Sure. But add some spice to the gig too. You don't need to tell poop jokes like Doc did, but you could bring a joke book and teach the kids some clean jokes. And have the kids play a game like Simon Says that would get them moving."

I crossed my arms. "Before Doc came along, Lucy and Mikey Sweet were perfectly happy with my books and educational games. So were their parents. And I'm not sure I should take babysitting advice from someone who hates kids."

"*Hate* is too strong a word. I don't hate kids. I despise them," Piper said. "I was just trying to help you so you can make enough money to buy a gorgeous dress for the eighth-grade dance."

"I'm not going," I said. "I'm not a good dancer. And I have nothing to wear. I grew out of my nice dresses and don't have money for a new one and—"

"Stop," Piper said. "Don't be afraid to take a risk. Maybe the dance will be the worst night of our lives, but maybe it'll be the best night of our lives. We'll never know if we don't go."

She had a point. I wanted a better social life, like my sister had. I sure wouldn't get it by avoiding social events. I looked at Piper and said, "Okay. I'll go to the dance."

Piper smiled. "It'll be fun."

"Or horrible," I said.

The bell rang, so Piper and I reluctantly left the cafeteria.

"Heads up!" Harrison Knox called a nano-second before a basketball hit my stomach and bounced off of it.

I grabbed the ball and glared at Harrison. He was wearing a 76ers basketball jersey, basketball shorts, and a cocky grin.

"Sorry about that," he said. But he didn't sound very sorry.

"Are you okay?" Piper asked me.

"I'm mad," I said.

"Toss me the ball," Harrison said.

I kept it. "You need to be more careful. You could have seriously injured someone."

"Yeah, yeah," he said, as if he couldn't care less. "Give me the ball back."

I hurled it as hard as I could. Unfortunately, that wasn't hard at all. The ball traveled a few feet, bounced a bit, and rolled in Harrison's direction.

Harrison scooped up the ball and said, "Next time, put more energy in your throw."

"Next time . . ." I tried to think of a great comeback. "Just . . . just . . . *argh!*"

That was not a great comeback. Or even a good comeback. It was, in fact, a terrible one.

"*Argh?*" Piper said.

I sighed. "Let's get out of here."

We walked to English class. Unfortunately, it was the only class Piper and I had together. Even more unfortunately, Ms. Roach was our teacher. I loved to read and I usually liked English, but not this year with Ms. Roach. I wouldn't have wished her on my worst enemy, let alone my best friend. Ms. Roach was long-winded, spoke in a mono-tone, and didn't have anything interesting to say. On the bright side, she could cure insomnia.

I always tried hard to pay attention in class, but my mind had a mind of its own, one that wandered. Piper, who sat on my left, didn't even try. She usually sketched pictures or wrote me notes or did anything but pay attention. The girl in front of me always texted during class, holding her phone on her lap. The boy on my right was Harrison. *Argh*. He usually looked at basketball cards hidden in his textbook or whispered jokes about our teacher.

Today's topic was run-on sentences. Ms. Roach said, "There are many disadvantages of run-on sentences—sentences that are much too long—the chief one of which is boring your reader with unnecessary words and exces-sive sentence length, but there are also other disadvantages, such as confusing your reader so that you fail to get your point or points across in a concise and . . ."

My eyelids felt very heavy.

Harrison whispered, "Ms. Roach is so boring she can't even entertain a doubt."

I put my hand over my mouth to stifle my giggles. I tried to distract myself by looking around the classroom.

Dominic Carelli was staring at me from across the room.

I looked down. My jeans were zipped and I didn't notice any food or stains on my clothes.

I glanced at Dominic again. He was still staring at me. Why?

I looked over at Piper. She'd let me know if I had something wrong with me. But she was busy drawing on a sheet of notebook paper. She had sketched a handsome man and pretty woman surrounded by three children. She was probably working on my babysitting flyer. Good. She was an awesome artist.

I craned my neck to see closer. The children had devil's horns and long, sharp fangs. A speech bubble by the man's mouth said, "Help us!" The woman's speech bubble said, "Our terrible kids are killing us!" In big letters underneath the drawing, Piper had written, "Quit yer belly-achin'! Call Kaitlyn!"

Oh, no. I knew Piper meant well, but there was no way I would hand out that flyer.

"Kaitlyn, what's wrong with your neck?" Harrison whispered.

"I'm fine," I whispered back. "Just bored."

"Bored?" Ms. Roach asked. She walked over to my desk.

Yikes. Either I'd whispered too loudly or Ms. Roach had supersonic hearing. Either way, I was in trouble.

"No talking in class, Harrison and Kaitlyn," the teacher said.

"I wasn't talking. I was whispering. Only one of us was talking," Harrison said, pointing to me.

"Also, no drawing in class." Ms. Roach snatched the flyer from Piper's desk and said, "Kaitlyn, Harrison, and Piper: In addition to your regular homework, you will each give me a list of sentences using em-dashes, colons, and semicolons correctly. Ten sentences for each type of punctuation. And work independently."

Piper shrugged and whispered, "What's an em-dash?"

Harrison said, "Kaitlyn, you're always getting everyone in trouble."

Some of my classmates laughed. They knew I never got anyone in trouble. I never even got myself in trouble. Until today.

I glared at Harrison. If looks could kill, he would have been a dead man.

Hadn't he done enough to me today? He'd hurled a basketball at me, mocked my throwing skills or lack thereof, gotten Ms. Roach mad at me, and humiliated me in front of my classmates.

Once class ended, I rushed over to Harrison and said, "Thanks a lot! You got me in trouble and made everyone laugh at me."

Harrison rolled his eyes. "You got yourself in trouble. And they were laughing at me."

"You may think you're a comedian, but I think you're a joke," I said.

"Can't I be both?" he said.

"What?" I asked.

"Both a comedian and a joke." He laughed and walked away.

Argh!

Sitter Smarts

Babysitters should reject jobs if they don't think they can handle them.

Chapter 3

I left my house on Saturday wearing a white collared shirt, black knee-length skirt, and black flats. I thought I looked pretty professional. I took along my phone and a thick stack of flyers.

I'd used Piper's artwork without the speech bubbles and devil's horns and fangs and added text: "Parents and children approve of Kaitlyn Perez, a very responsible local babysitter. I'll keep your precious children safe and sound while you enjoy a well-deserved evening out." I'd put my cell phone number on the bottom of the flyer.

Our next-door neighbor was childless, so I walked past her house. I passed by the next house too, which had teenagers. I stopped at the third house because I'd seen young boys playing outside. I knocked on the door, but got no answer. I slipped a flyer under the mat and moved on to the next house. No answer there either.

I walked and walked. Most people didn't come to their door. Other people said they didn't have young children or didn't need a sitter.

About two blocks from my house, a woman with messy hair and weary eyes came to the door. A cute little boy who looked about three years old clung to her leg. I smiled and said, "I'm Kaitlyn Perez, and I'd like to babysit for you."

The woman said, "I'm Heather Doyle, and I could use a sitter. How much do you charge?"

I handed her a flyer and told her my rate.

She shook her head. "Too much for me."

"My rates are flexible," I said.

"I could give you half that," she said.

Half! That was terrible! Still, Heather Doyle was the first person interested in my services today. And her child looked sweet. Babysitting for him would be easy.

Inside the house, a girl called out, "Mommy!"

"Mommy, mommy, mommy, mommy, mommy, mommy, mommy," another girl whined.

A boy who must have been the three-year-old's twin ran toward us, banging loudly on a toy drum.

"How many children do you have?" I asked.

"Four," she said. "And a baby."

I had an urge to scream, "I'm not that desperate for a job!" snatch my flyer from the woman's hand, and flee as fast as I could.

Instead, I took a deep breath and said, "Mrs. Doyle, I won't halve my hourly rate to watch more than double the number of children I usually sit for. Thank you anyway."

"Please . . . can you babysit today?"

I shook my head.

Inside the house, a baby started crying. The girls kept whining for their mommy.

"Tomorrow? Or the next day?" Mrs. Doyle asked desperately.

I said loudly and slowly, "The rate you're offering is too low."

"A day next week?" she asked as the twins started wrestling over the toy drum.

I turned and walked away.

Mrs. Doyle yelled, "You can babysit here anytime you want!"

I picked up my pace and didn't look back.

I went to eight more houses before someone finally answered the door. "Hello," an elderly woman said.

I smiled at her. "Hello, I'm Kaitlyn Perez. I'm a very responsible and experienced babysitter. I wonder if you—"

She interrupted me. "Dear, even my grandchildren are too old to need a babysitter."

"Oh. Well, I—"

"What I really need is a nurse," she said. "I have shingles. There's a line of angry blisters around my torso. Very painful."

"I'm sorry to have bothered—"

"They have lingered for weeks now." After describing her shingles in further detail, she told me about her gum disease and her toenail fungus.

When she finally took a breath, I handed her a flyer and said, "If you know anyone who needs a babysit—"

"My neighbor does," she said.

"Great!" I said. "I can go to your neighbor's house and introduce myself today."

"She's just a block down," the woman said. "I'd go with you, but, according to my podiatrist, I have plantar fasciitis in my feet. It's a very painful foot condition."

Then she went on about the pain in her feet for a long time.

Finally, I said, "If you can point out her house, I'll walk over there."

"Whose house? My podiatrist's?"

"The person who needs a sitter," I said.

"My podiatrist doesn't need a sitter," the woman said. "Oh, you mean the neighbor I was telling you about before. Her name is Heather Doyle. She has five children."

I tried hard not to scream, but a little choking noise escaped from my mouth.

"You don't sound well. I get a cough like that sometimes. Just last week it was so bad I almost coughed up a lung. The phlegm goes—"

I interrupted her. "I'd better go. Keep the babysitting flyer."

"I'll put it next to the one I got yesterday."

My stomach sank. "Someone else passed out babysitting flyers?"

The woman nodded. "Along with a little bag of delicious cookies he baked. I shouldn't have eaten them. I get allergic reactions: hives, blotches, swelling, rash—"

"He?" I asked.

"Pardon? My hearing isn't very good. I've got wax buildup in my ears and—"

"The babysitter is male?"

"Yes." She smiled. "A very nice young man."

I felt my eyes narrow. A nasty, job-stealing young man.

"He said to call him Doc." She thrust her face close to mine. "Does this mole look suspicious to you?"

"No." I hurried away before she could tell me more about any other medical issues.

I knocked at the house next door, but got no answer. When I put my flyer under the mat, I noticed another flyer there, stapled to a plastic bag of cookies. The flyer said, "Kids love Doc! Best babysitter in the neighborhood!" Underneath was a phone number.

I was the best babysitter in the neighborhood! I wanted to tear up the flyer, smash the cookies, call the phone number, and yell at Doc for stealing my business. But I was too wimpy to do any of those things.

Instead, I hurried off and kept knocking on doors. The few people who answered didn't need or want a sitter. My shoulders slumped and my pace slowed. My feet were killing me. Maybe I needed to see a podiatrist too.

About a mile from my house, my knock was answered—by Harrison Knox. "Hey there, Kaitlyn." He smirked. "How did you track down my address?"

"I didn't know you lived here," I said through gritted teeth. "I'm passing out flyers to get baby-sitting jobs. See?" I thrust a flyer at him.

He looked at the flyer. "So you came here to give me your phone number? Sneaky."

"No." I rolled my eyes. "I am *so* not in the mood for your jokes, Harrison. I've had a long day. I knocked on a bunch of doors with no luck."

"Sorry. Do you want to come in and wait out the rain?"

I shook my head. "It's not raining."

"It's supposed to rain any minute now."

"I'll be fine," I said. "Hey, did another babysitter come to your door yesterday? Apparently, he handed out flyers and cookies."

"As far as I know, you're the only babysitter who's come here to 'hand out flyers.'" He made air quotes around the last words, as if I hadn't really come to his house to hand out flyers.

I ignored him and asked, "Do you know a guy named Doc?"

Harrison shook his head.

"Well, bye." I turned to leave.

"It's looking really gray out there, like the clouds are about to burst," he said. "You sure you don't want to hang out here for a while? Or I could ask my mom to drive you home."

"I'm fine!" I said.

"You want to borrow an umbrella?"

"It's not raining!" I shouted before hurrying away.

The rain came a minute later.

A minute after that, it started pouring.

I was still a few blocks from home when the hail began.

Sitter Smarts

Babysitters should have the cell
phone numbers of the kids' parents
and a neighbor or two.

Chapter 4

"What are you doing this weekend?" Piper asked me before biting into the ham and cheese quesadilla I'd brought to school.

I frowned. "I'll tell you what I'm not doing: I'm not babysitting."

It was a sunny Friday afternoon and I was with my best friend, eating delicious prepackaged meat and cheese slices and crackers. But I still felt ornery. In the four days since I'd plastered my neighborhood with flyers, I'd gotten babysitting offers from exactly zero people. Anyone needing a sitter had probably called Doc. I had Googled combinations of "Doc," "babysitter," and "Fairview," the name of our town. But that didn't help me figure out who Doc was.

Old-fashioned reasoning had proved more effective, leading me to Dominic Carelli. Removing the middle letters—*M-I-N-I*—from the name Dominic left the name Doc. And he was always staring at me in English class, probably while he schemed up new, devious ways to hog all the babysitting jobs. I couldn't prove Dominic was really Doc—not yet—but he was a highly likely suspect.

"I bet Doc is feeding all the neighborhood children junky homemade cookies that will rot their teeth and playing games that will rile them up and destroy their houses," I said. "Not that I'm bitter."

"You sound bitter. You've sounded bitter all week," Piper said.

"You're right. I'm sorry for being such a . . ." I tried to think of the right word.

"Debbie Downer? Sullen Sarah? Whiny Wendy?" Piper suggested.

"Okay. I get it."

Piper grinned. "Crabby Cassie, Testy Tessa, Grouchy Gabby, Unbearable Ursula?"

I laughed and Piper joined in.

"I need to get out. I've been stewing in my room all week," I said. "Just call me Stewing Stephanie."

"Let's walk to the mall after school," Piper said. "The mall will make you feel better."

"Good idea." Fairview Mall was my favorite place, after the library. It was also Piper's favorite, after the zoo.

After school, I stood in an empty hallway and called my mother to ask for a ride home from the mall.

"What do you need from there?" she asked.

"Some cheering up," I said through the lump in my throat.

"*Mija*," she said. That was Spanish for "my daughter." "What's wrong?" Mom's voice was soft and soothing, the same tone she used with her social services clients.

"Everything's wrong. I can't find a new baby-sitting job, my English teacher is boring, and two of the boys in my class are really annoying. I'm completely stressed out."

"That's it?" My mother asked, her tone no longer soft or soothing. "The girl I saw this morning shares a one-bedroom apartment with her grandmother and little brothers. She has a reason to be stressed out. *La vida no es un camino de roses*." That meant that life wasn't a bed of roses.

In other words, my mom thought I was a whiner.

"I guess I have it good," I said, but the lump in my throat had gotten bigger. "So, can you drive me and Piper home from the mall?"

"I'll pick you up on my way home from work."

"Okay, thanks." I hung up. I told myself that I was lucky. But the lump throbbed hard in my throat.

Piper cheered me up on the way to the mall. As we walked, Piper and I told each other silly jokes. Our favorite was: What's brown and sticky? A stick. We were both laughing when we reached the mall.

We went to the pet supply store first. We looked at sweaters for Piper's dog, which we both found totally adorable, and rocks for her aquarium, which Piper found fascinating and I did not.

As we left the store, Piper said, "Let's shop for your dress for the eighth-grade dance."

I shook my head. "The little bit of money I saved from babysitting has to go toward my cell phone bill."

"Won't your parents buy a new dress for you?" Piper asked. "My mom bought me a pretty one last week."

"That's because you pretended you wanted to wear a crop top and tight miniskirt to the dance. Genius move on your part," I said.

Piper grinned. "I had to sit through my parents' long lecture about dressing appropriately. But it was worth it."

"If I tried that, my parents would buy me something awful. Like a super cheap dress with pink and purple polka-dots that went out of style in the last millennium."

"So what are you going to wear to the dance?" Piper asked.

I shrugged. "None of my old dresses fit."

"Well, maybe we'll find a nice new dress on sale. Or maybe you'll get a babysitting job soon."

"Maybe," I said.

We walked through the mall, stopping at a few stores. We saw a lot of pretty dresses, but even the ones on sale were expensive.

I spotted a gorgeous dress in the window of a boutique store called Just for Teens. I stopped and stared at it. It was red with a fitted top, capped sleeves, and a flared short skirt. Lace and sequins topped the entire dress.

Piper stopped next to me. "What are you staring—ooh!" she squealed.

"I love that dress!" I exclaimed.

"Me too! And red goes so well with your dark hair. Try it on."

"I doubt it's on sale," I said.

"I'll check." Piper ran into the store.

I followed her. The store smelled strongly of meat and grease and onions.

"Excuse me," Piper said to the salesclerk, who was sitting behind the counter and holding a half-eaten hamburger. "My friend would like to try on the red dress shown in the store window."

Using her burger-free hand the clerk pointed to a rack with a few red dresses on it.

"Is the dress on sale?" I asked.

The salesclerk shrugged and took another bite of her burger.

Piper rushed to the rack and held up the dress. "Kaitlyn, they have it in your size. It's so gorgeous!"

"I know. But how much is it?" I asked.

She looked at the tag and frowned.

"It costs a fortune, doesn't it?"

She brought the dress over to me. "Just try it on. It might not even look good on you."

The salesclerk unlocked a fitting room with one hand while still holding her burger in the other, a pretty impressive feat.

"Try it on!" Piper thrust the dress at me.

I kept my hands at my sides.

"Come on." Piper kept shoving the dress at me.

Finally, surrendering to Piper and the dazzling red beauty of the dress, I went into the fitting room and closed the door.

I looked at the price tag. Ouch! The dress cost much more than my parents would be willing to spend. It cost much more than I'd be willing to spend, even if I had my steady babysitting job. In order for me to even consider buying the dress, it would have to be the most amazing dress ever in the history of the universe.

I tried it on. It was the most amazing dress ever in the history of the universe. It fit me perfectly, as if it had been expertly tailored just for me. Piper had been right about the color. The bright red not only made my hair look shinier, it made my teeth whiter, my skin softer, and my body curvier. And the dress's short-but-not-too-short length made my legs seem long and shapely. The sequins added drama while the lace added a delicate touch. This was the absolute perfect dress for me.

"Can I see it?" Piper asked from the other side of the fitting room door.

I opened the door.

Piper stared at me wide-eyed. "You look amazing! I knew you would."

"I love it! I just wish I could afford it. My parents wouldn't even pay half what this dress costs." I sighed, giving myself one last look in the mirror. "Well, time to change from a gorgeous goddess back into a normal person."

"Wait. Let me take a picture of you in your gorgeous goddess-ness."

I gave Piper my phone. Piper's parents had taken hers away months ago, telling her she'd get it back once she got all As and Bs. Given Piper's attitude about school, she'd be without a phone until graduation—if she managed to graduate.

I smiled while Piper snapped pictures of me.

"Keep those pictures on your phone," she said. "Every time you look at them, you'll be inspired to earn money for the dress."

"Great idea," I said.

I reluctantly changed back to my T-shirt and jeans and normal-person status.

Piper and I roamed the mall again. I looked at other dresses halfheartedly, but none of them compared to the beautiful red one I'd tried on. We went to a gadget store and took turns using its chair massager. Then we hung out in the bookstore, sitting on the rug and leafing through magazines.

"None of the dresses in these magazines are as pretty as the one you tried on," Piper said.

"I know. I love that dress so much." I reached into the front pocket of my purse for my phone, so I could compare the picture of the red dress to the pictures in the magazine. But my phone wasn't there.

I panicked for a moment, before remembering that Piper had used my phone. "Piper, you forgot to give me back my phone," I said.

Piper put her hands in her front pants pockets, then in her back pockets. She came up empty. She asked in a shaky voice, "Are you sure I didn't give it back to you?"

"Positive. I always keep my phone in the front pocket of my purse. You know how organized I am."

"And you know how disorganized I am." Piper said. "Wait . . . I just realized I left your phone in the Just for Teens store, on the bench outside the fitting room." She stood and hurried out of the bookstore. I followed her, running through the mall, dodging the shoppers.

We were out of breath by the time we returned to Just for Teens. The same salesclerk was there, sitting behind the counter again. The store still smelled like a burger joint.

"I left a cell—" Piper panted. "A cell—" Pant. "I left a—"

"She left my cell phone in here," I told the clerk. "Did you see it?"

The clerk shook her head.

Piper ran to the bench by the fitting room, but there was nothing on it. She crawled on the rug and looked underneath bench.

"Maybe it's on the rug somewhere," I said, pacing the store and staring down at the rug.

Piper asked the clerk, "Did other customers come in since we left?"

The clerk shrugged. "A few."

Piper and I searched all over the store, but we couldn't find my phone.

"It might be in the mall's Lost and Found," the clerk said.

"If a customer found it, wouldn't they have told you instead of just going to the Lost and Found?" Piper asked.

The clerk shrugged again.

Piper gave her our home phone numbers, in case the cell phone turned up. Then we walked to the Lost and Found, but no one had turned in a phone.

"My new phone," I said in a choked voice. "There's no way I can afford another one."

"I think maybe the salesclerk took it. She kept avoiding my eyes, like she was guilty of something." Piper said. "I'm so sorry, Kaitlyn. If I had any money, I'd buy you a new phone myself."

"Why don't you get money?" My voice came out too loud and too angry.

I clamped my mouth shut. Piper hadn't lost my phone on purpose. She just hadn't thought about it.

Still, she knew how much my phone meant to me. I loved my phone. I had worked so hard for it. And it had been Piper's idea to borrow it to take my picture.

"Piper, how could you do this to me?" I blurted out, my voice still loud and angry.

"You act like I murdered a kitten. I just forgot to give your phone back to you, that's all."

I crossed my arms. "And you left my phone in the store. And you tried to convince me to buy a dress I couldn't afford." The words tumbled from my mouth like a dangerous avalanche. "And you got me in trouble with Ms. Roach by drawing that really dumb babysitting flyer."

"What's really dumb is for me to stand in the middle of the mall while you insult me. I'm leaving," Piper said.

I shook my head. "How are you going to get home without a ride from my mom?"

"I'll walk home," she said, her voice cracking on "walk."

Hearing how upset she sounded and picturing her walking home by herself shrank my anger. In a much calmer voice, I said, "Your house is like three miles away."

Piper crossed her arms. "I'd rather spend an hour walking than one more minute hearing you blame me for everything."

"It's not my fault you took my phone and then lost it," I said.

She shook her head, turned away, and walked toward the mall exit.

I stared after her. I'd lost my job, my phone, and my best friend. And I had no idea how to get any of them back.

Sitter Smarts

Babysitters should keep
children happy and
houses tidy.

Chapter 5

I called Mrs. Doyle as soon as I got home from the mall. I would have called her from the mall, but I no longer had a cell phone. Actually, that wasn't true; I wouldn't have called her at all if I had a cell phone. After all, I wouldn't have needed to buy a new one.

When I offered to babysit, Mrs. Doyle yelped happily, as if I'd just agreed to donate my kidney. She asked me to come over that night. So there I was a few hours later, in the boys' bedroom, changing Ethan or Evan's diaper. I wasn't sure which twin was which. They looked exactly alike. Neither of them was potty-trained, and to make things worse, they both had diarrhea. Oh, joy.

Still, I told myself that there were worse places to spend an evening than the Doyles' house. But it took me a while to think of any such places. I finally came up with a jail cell or a hospital bed.

While I stood at the changing table, four-year-old Lauren yelled from the kitchen, "I want a popsicle!"

"Me too! I'll get them," six-year-old Madison said.

"No popsicles!" I called out.

"Popsicle!" the boy on the changing table said.

"No popsicles," I repeated. "They're bad for you and they're messy."

"Popsicle! Popsicle! Popsicle!" the boy on the changing table yelled.

If my hands hadn't just wiped his bottom, I would have clapped them over my ears.

Then Lauren said, "Uh-oh."

I did not like the sound of that. "What's wrong?" I asked as I fastened Ethan or Evan's clean diaper.

"The mouse!" Madison screamed. "It's running through the kitchen!"

Her screams woke the baby. He screamed even louder than his sisters.

I finished changing Ethan or Evan's diaper, quickly washed my hands, and plucked the baby from his crib. Then I headed to the kitchen to capture the mouse.

On the way, the baby stopped screaming. He spit up all over my shirt. Then he resumed his screaming.

I felt like screaming myself. Instead, I grabbed a diaper wipe and cleaned his face. I'd clean my shirt whenever I had a spare moment—if I ever had a spare moment.

The other twin grabbed my leg. "I just did another poopy," he said.

"Kaitlyn! The mouse is on the kitchen table!" Madison shouted.

"Okay, okay," I said. "I'll get rid of the mouse. Then I'll change your diaper, Evan."

"I'm Ethan, not Evan," the boy said. "And I got poopy running down my leg."

Jail cells and hospital beds were sounding better and better.

I changed Ethan's diaper and cleaned up his leg and my hands. Then I strapped the baby into his swing and walked into the kitchen.

Lauren sat at the kitchen table. Tears were streaming down her cheeks.

"Don't worry, Lauren," I said. "I'll get the mouse out of your house. It will never, ever bother you again."

"You big meanie, Kaitlyn!" she sobbed.

"The mouse is our pet. He got out of his cage," Madison explained.

"Oh. Oops. Sorry." I hugged Lauren while I wondered how on Earth I was going to get the mouse back in its cage.

Piper would know how. For many years she had owned Chester, her dear, departed rat. But I couldn't call her, not after our fight at the mall today. I'd have to figure out mouse-catching myself. *Ugh.*

I thought for a minute before telling Madison to bring the mouse's empty cage into the kitchen. Then I opened cupboard doors until I found a large plastic bowl. I tiptoed to the kitchen table and tried to pull the bowl over the mouse. I missed.

I tried again. And again. And again. After about fifty attempts, I finally managed to get the bowl over the mouse.

I moved its cage next to the bowl. When I lifted the bowl a little, the mouse scampered out, right into its cage. I quickly shut the door and breathed a huge sigh of relief. Problem solved.

Many more problems were left, though. I cleaned more spit-up and poop, broke up arguments, put away toys, bathed the kids, repeated a zillion times that they couldn't have popsicles, got everyone ready for bed, told them to go to bed, ordered them to go to bed, pleaded with them to go to bed, and silently vowed to never, ever, ever set foot in the Doyles' house again.

A few minutes after the last Doyle child had finally fallen asleep, Mr. and Mrs. Doyle arrived home. Their steps were light, their faces were happy, and their pay was measly.

I stuffed the money into my purse, grabbed my babysitting bag, which I'd been too busy to even open, and hurried to the front door.

Mrs. Doyle slowly sauntered after me, as if she wanted to keep me there as long as possible.

As she drove me home, she did not ask me how my evening went. She obviously knew how an evening with her two children, two toddlers, and baby would have gone—not well.

"Can you come back tomorrow night?" she asked me.

I shook my head. "Sorry. No."

"The next night?"

"No."

"The night after that? Or any night at all?"

"No," I said firmly.

"How about a morning or afternoon?"

"Mrs. Doyle, your kids are adorable," I said. "But they're a little too much for me. I'm sorry. I won't be babysitting for you again."

She let out a long, loud sigh. I felt bad for her, but I had to look out for myself. Watching the Doyle kids was bad for my health—physical, mental, spiritual, and all other kinds of health.

I rushed out of the car as soon as we got to my house. My parents opened the front door for me and asked how my evening went.

"Not good," I said. "Don't worry if you hear screaming tonight. I'll just be having nightmares about crying babies, whining children, toddler diarrhea, and mice."

I hurried to my room, sat on my bed, put my babysitting bag down next to me, and took a few deep breaths.

Ahh. Finally. Peace and quiet and a soft, lovely comforter.

Then the front door slammed.

My sister stomped through the house and stormed into my room. "Look at me!" she demanded.

I looked at her.

I covered my mouth, but I couldn't help laughing.

Eve was covered head to toe—or rather red comb to webbed orange feet—in a giant, bright, feathered, and horribly hideous chicken costume.

She scowled and sank next to me on my bed.

I stopped laughing. "Please take your grimy feathers off my spotless new comforter," I said.

Eve moved to my desk chair. "Did I ever mention I hate my job?" she said. "Hate, hate, hate it!"

"You've mentioned it a few hundred times. Did you have to wear that horrendous costume for the entire party?" I asked.

"Yes. Those were the longest four hours of my life. When my boss originally hired me and told me I'd be wearing costumes, I figured he meant princess costumes." Eve shook her head. "The last four weeks, I've had to dress as a beach ball, a penguin, a sunflower, and now a giant chicken. This chicken costume is the worst. I couldn't even go to the bathroom, because it would take too long to get this monstrosity off and on again. Not only that, but I had to say 'Bawk' at the end of every sentence."

"Huh?" I asked as I picked up the feathers that had fallen onto my comforter.

"When I was painting kids' faces, I had to say, 'Do you want a butterfly or a horse? Bawk.' Then they'd tell me, and I'd have to ask, 'What color? Bawk.'" She shuddered. "Imagine how annoying that got. I had the most horrible night in the history of the world."

I shook my head. "There is no way that is true. *I* had the most horrible night in the history of the world. I babysat four little kids, a baby, and a mouse. And none of them behaved. Especially not the mouse."

"At least you got to wear your own clothes. Can you help me get this horrible thing off of me before I pee in it?" Eve asked.

"I'd be happy to. I don't want you peeing in my bedroom." I unzipped the back of her costume and asked, "Could you get me a job at the party company you work for?"

Eve stared at me with her eyebrows raised. "You're either nuts or you haven't heard one thing I told you since I started my job. I've been working really hard, wearing embarrassing costumes, and making very little money. The party company is a terrible employer."

"Maybe, but I'm desperate for money!" I said, wishing for the zillionth time that Piper hadn't lost my phone.

"You'd have to be desperate to work there. But you also have to be sixteen," Eve said. "Gotta go pee." She ran off.

I sighed and picked up my babysitting bag so I could return it to my closet.

A thick, bright purple liquid dripped from the bag. Underneath the bag, a purple puddle spread on my comforter—my beautiful, expensive comforter.

I blinked back tears and looked inside the bag. It was full of melting purple popsicles. The Doyle children must have put them there. The popsicles had dripped all over my board games and books, through the bag, and onto my bed.

I could probably salvage the games, but I'd have to pay for the damage to the library books, and I doubted I could get out the purple stain from my comforter. I blinked and blinked, but could no longer stop the tears from streaming down my face.

Sitter Smarts

Babysitters should be kind
and compassionate.

Chapter 6

It was Monday, which meant I had a full week of school ahead of me. What I did not have was a phone, money, a job, or a best friend. I thought about staying in bed all day, but lying under my ruined comforter was making me miserable. Besides, I didn't want to ruin my perfect attendance record.

So I went to school. I spent all morning on the alert for Piper, hoping I wouldn't run into her, but also sort of hoping I would run into her.

I didn't see Piper until lunchtime. She sat at our regular table, looking around the cafeteria. I wondered whether she did or did not hope to run into me. She waved at me, a half smile on her face.

I waved back at her, a full smile on my face. Phew. Our friendship had survived the biggest fight we'd ever had. Sure, Piper had been careless with my phone, but I'd reacted so badly. It was time to make up.

Two girls from the middle-school band rushed past me. "Piper! Thanks for waving us over," one of them said.

"What's new, Piper?" the other girl asked.

Piper sure hadn't wasted time replacing me. I turned away and headed to Jenna Burkhart and Rose Lopez's table. I'd eaten with them a few times when Piper was absent from school. Jenna, Rose, and I had been neighbors since we were little kids. We used to hang out a lot, mostly playing tetherball in front of my house or riding scooters around the neighborhood. Jenna and Rose were still best friends with each other, but I was more of an acquaintance now. It wasn't really anyone's fault. As divorcing celebrities liked to say, we'd "grown apart." In English, that meant that a couple of years ago, Jenna and Rose had stopped playing tetherball because they didn't want to break their fingernails, and quit riding their scooters because they thought it made them look dorky. So even though we lived close to each other, I hardly ever saw them around the neighborhood anymore.

They smiled and said hello as I sat with them. "We were just debating whose mother is worse," Rose said. "My mom won't let me wear high heels. She's so mean."

"Mine won't let me dye my hair," Jenna said, flipping her long brown hair back.

"I think your hair is pretty the way it is," I said.

Jenna shook her head. "I need to be blond. Guys like girls with blond hair the best. It's been statistically proven and everything."

"And they like girls with long legs. High heels make people's legs look longer. I need to wear high heels," Rose said.

"Your moms sound like evil monsters," I joked.

"I know!" Jenna exclaimed.

"They're so awful!" Rose said.

They must not have realized I was joking.

"We were also debating who's the cutest guy in eighth grade," Jenna said. "I think it's A. J. Lundy. He has amazing cheekbones and midnight eyes."

"He's cute," Rose said. "But Dominic Carelli is cuter. His hair is *sooo* thick and his eyes are *sooo* big."

"You know who else has thick hair and big eyes? A gorilla," I joked. Rose and Jenna frowned. They didn't get my jokes at all.

Piper would have laughed at that. I looked over at our table. Piper was sitting with the two girls from band. They were all laughing. Piper used to play drums in the band, but she got kicked out after doing a really cool—but totally unauthorized—rock solo during a concert. I smiled as I remembered that.

"Pay attention, Kaitlyn," Rose said.

I looked away from Piper. "Huh?"

"We asked who you think is cutest, A. J. or Dominic?" Jenna said.

"They're both very cute," I said. "But Dominic acts weird. Does he ever stare at you?"

They shook their heads.

"Do you know if Dominic's nickname is Doc?" I asked.

"I don't know. But his nickname should be Hot Stuff," Rose said.

"*Ooh-la-la!*" Jenna said.

I rolled my eyes. Then I looked at Piper again. She was leaning in to chat with the girls at our table, as if she'd suddenly become best friends with them.

I leaned in to chat with Jenna and Rose. But I couldn't think of anything to say.

"Are you feeling all right?" Jenna asked me.

"Your head is hanging over my sandwich," Rose said.

I lifted my head—and saw Harrison standing over me.

"Hi, Harrison," Jenna said. Then she giggled, even though no one had told a joke.

"Hello, Harrison." Rose batted her eyelashes.

I rolled my eyes again.

"Hey, Kaitlyn," Harrison said.

"Harrison, are you stalking me?" I asked.

I waited for his wisecrack in return. He was always making wisecracks. But not today. His shoulders were hunched, and he was frowning slightly. He looked as miserable as I felt. "Can I talk to you, Kaitlyn?" he asked.

"Fine," I said, sounding about as enthusiastic as a rock.

"I mean, can we talk in private?" he asked.

"Ooh!" Jenna giggled again.

Rose smacked her lips.

I rolled my eyes once again. I'd rolled them so much the last few minutes that they were starting to get tired.

Then I got up from the lunch table and walked out of the cafeteria, with Harrison following me. I stopped under a tree a few yards from the cafeteria. "What do you want, Harrison?"

"Well . . ." He blinked a bunch of times before looking away from me. "I . . ."

I'd never seen him so nervous. In fact, I'd never seen him at all nervous.

"I was wondering . . . Since you babysit . . ." More fast blinking. No eye contact. "Could you give me some babysitting tips? I'm thinking of trying it."

"You? Babysit?" I crossed my arms. "I wouldn't trust you to take care of a plant, let alone a baby. I hate to break it to you, but babysitting involves more than telling jokes and playing pranks."

"I know that." After a long pause, he said, "I could use the money."

I didn't say anything. I was waiting for him to make a dumb joke. But he didn't.

Finally, he asked, "So do you have any advice?"

Hmm . . . maybe he really did want advice. Well, he wouldn't get it from me. All I needed was another babysitter in the neighborhood competing with me. I already had more than enough competition from Dominic AKA Doc. I was not about to help Harrison get babysitter jobs.

Then I had a thought—an evil and ingenious thought. I acted on it.

"I know a family that needs a sitter," I said. "They live close to you. Maybe you know them. The Doyles?"

"No." Harrison's frown disappeared, replaced by an eager smile. He obviously had no idea that the Doyles were terrifying.

I felt a twinge of guilt, like a feather flitting around in my stomach. So I said, "They're a large family and they don't pay very well."

"No problem." Harrison tilted his chin up, as if a great guy like him could easily handle a large family. He was so arrogant. And he'd really acted like a jerk. He had beamed me with a basketball, gotten me in trouble in class, teased me about tracking down his address, and now wanted to compete with me for jobs. A few hours with the Doyle clan would humble him for months.

"The Doyles only have one sweet little pet, and the children are quiet and well-behaved. You'll love them," I said. I gave Harrison the Doyles' address.

"Thank you. That's really generous of you," Harrison said.

The twinge of guilt turned into a pang of guilt. The feather that had wafted around my stomach now felt more like a fast-flying bird.

"Do you have any advice for me about baby-sitting?" Harrison asked. "Besides taking an umbrella if it might rain?"

Argh! He was teasing me again! The bird in my stomach flew away.

"Bring stuff to do so you won't get bored while the Doyle children quietly play by themselves," I said.

"Glad to hear they entertain themselves. Do you have any more advice?" Harrison asked. But luckily, the bell rang, so I hurried away.

Once I got to English class, I avoided looking at both Harrison and Piper, fearing I'd laugh at him and glare at her. Instead, I tried to focus on the teacher.

"Today we will talk about clarity in writing," Ms. Roach said. "Essays should get one central point across. The most important thing about essays is that it has correct grammar. Make sure the subject of your sentences are in agreement with your verb. Writers should not meander when putting pen to page, which is an old expression meaning writing, which was used before the invention of the computer or even the typewriter, manual or electric . . ."

I stopped listening and glanced around the classroom. Piper was sketching playful kittens, as if she didn't have a care in the world, as if she couldn't care less that she'd lost her best friend.

I turned my head. Harrison was kicking a toy hockey puck back and forth with the kid next to him. He whispered to me, "Thanks again for the babysitting tip."

The Doyle children were going to eat him alive. The bird returned, pecking hard at my stomach.

I looked away. Dominic was staring at me again, smiling a bit. He was probably gloating about ruining my babysitting career.

I wanted to shout at him, "I know who you really are, Dominic, you job-stealing jerk! Stop looking at me!"

"Kaitlyn!" Ms. Roach said.

My classmates giggled.

Oops. I hadn't just *wanted* to shout at Dominic. I'd actually gone and done it.

"You cannot keep interrupting my class, Kaitlyn Perez," the teacher said. "You just got yourself detention after school today. I will notify your parents."

Sitter Smarts

If a babysitter can't control the children, she should call their parents.

Chapter 7

From my seat in the front row of the detention room, I watched my fellow delinquents trickle in after school. Most of them were boys, many looked angry, and none of them were my friends. A guy with a nose ring, a ripped T-shirt, and a stench of cigarettes sat next to me. Oh, joy.

Mr. Washington, the assistant principal, waved to him and said, "Hello again, Jack. You've become quite the regular around here. We must stop meeting like this." Then Mr. Washington took roll call and told us to keep quiet and stay seated. "I suggest you do homework," he said, "for once in your lives."

As I opened my math book, Jack leaned over and asked, "What are you in here for?"

I'd already gotten into enough trouble for talking in school. I put my index finger to my lip.

A minute later, Jack slid a note on my desk. It said, "I got caut smoking behind the scool. What did you do? Your cute."

I shook my head and stayed silent. The guy should have spent less time smoking and more time learning spelling and grammar.

I stared at my math book, but I couldn't focus. I looked around. The guy sitting in front of me thumbed through a catalog of tattoos. He flipped past the heart and Mom tattoos, stopping at a page full of swear words.

I stared at my math book again. I couldn't concentrate on the assigned chapters. I did other types of math in my head. I counted the many things that had gone wrong the last few weeks, calculated the large difference between the money I had and the amount I needed to pay my next phone bill, and estimated how many times my mother would tell me I'd disappointed her.

My mother started right away. I was getting in her car after detention when she said, "I'm very disappointed in you."

"You should be." The words struggled past the lump in my throat and ended up sounding like frog croaks.

"What's going on with you, Kaitlyn?"

"Nothing," I croaked. But, obviously, something was going on with me, something big, because I started sobbing as soon as we left the school parking lot.

Mom pulled over to the curb. She turned off the car, took off her seat belt, and hugged me. "Talk to me, Mija," she said.

I did. At first through sobs, then through sniffles and a few stray tears, I told my mother about losing my babysitting job, losing my phone, losing my best friend, and losing my marbles in class.

After I told my mom everything, I slid out of her arms and said, "I know you see kids every day who only have one pair of pants and sneakers they've outgrown and terrible parents. Compared with them, I have nothing to complain about. But even though I have first-world problems, they're still problems to me."

My mother nodded. "There are always people worse off than others. Even some foster children in America live like kings compared to starving children in Africa. I'm sorry I haven't given you more sympathy."

"I'm sorry I disrupted my class today."

"Don't do that again," Mom said, smiling at me and squeezing my shoulder gently.

"I won't," I said. "Can we go home now?"

Mom nodded, put her seat belt back on, and turned on the ignition. "I'll buy you a dress for the eighth-grade dance. How about that cute orange and green striped one we saw on sale at the discount store last week?"

I frowned. The bright polyester dress my mother liked was many things—unfashionable, unflattering, ugly—but by no stretch of the imagination was it "cute."

Finally I said, "Thanks for the offer, Mom, but it's not my style."

"May I offer you some advice about Piper?" she asked.

"Is it that I should call her and apologize?" I asked. "Because I'm going to do that as soon as we get home."

Mom squeezed my shoulder again. "I guess you don't need my advice, Mija."

Just thinking about talking to Piper again made me feel better. The lump that had lived in my throat since our fight was still there, because making the phone call wouldn't be easy and I wasn't sure Piper would accept my apology. But the lump was smaller.

I closed my eyes and tried to compose a great apology. First, I decided, I should tell Piper how much I valued her friendship. I could recite some famous quotes about friendship. I'd have to look them up before I called, because I didn't know any offhand.

The car slowed and my mom said, "*Sal de la vida es la amistad*," meaning, "Friendship is the spice of life."

"How did you know I needed a friendship quote?" I asked her.

"I didn't. Look who's here."

I opened my eyes—and saw Piper standing on our porch.

My throat lump disappeared. Warmth spread through my body. I forgot about composing a great apology. Instead, I ran over to Piper and said, "I'm sorry I acted so nasty about my phone!"

"I'm sorry for being so irresponsible."

"It happens to everyone," I told her. "I was so irresponsible, I ruined my comforter and my babysitting bag."

"Oh, Kaitlyn. That's awful!" Piper said.

I shrugged. "That was nothing compared to almost ruining our friendship."

"I hope this helps." Piper reached into her pants pocket and pulled out a phone. It looked a lot like my lost phone. She handed it to me.

I turned it on. It was my phone. "Thank you! You're the best! How did you ever find it?" I exclaimed.

"Finding it was the easy part. I knew where it was. Getting it was harder. I went back to Just for Teens after school today and ordered the store clerk to give back your phone."

"But on Saturday she said she hadn't seen it."

"On Saturday, Sweetcakes wasn't with me." Piper grinned. "Owning a five-foot-long king snake sure can come in handy. He scared the clerk half to death."

"You always told me Sweetcakes wouldn't hurt a fly," I said.

"Yes, Sweetcakes is a total sweetheart. But I didn't tell the store clerk that. I said that my snake's name was Killer and that he loved to eat human flesh."

I laughed.

"You should have seen it! She handed over your phone so fast," Piper said.

"She probably would have handed over her wallet and first-born child too," I said.

Piper nodded. "I got her to promise to sell you that gorgeous red dress at her employee discount, which is forty percent off."

I reached out to hug her. Then I stopped. "You don't have Sweetcakes with you now, do you?"

Piper shook her head. "Sweetcakes is resting in his cage now."

Phew! I hugged Piper hard.

She added, "He's always so exhausted after eating a live mouse." I tried not to gag.

We went inside my house. The first thing I did was charge my phone. Then I brought a large bag of potato chips into my room, sat on my comforter, and opened the bag.

Piper stood at the entrance to my room. "What in the world are you doing?" she asked.

"What in the world do you think I'm doing? Eating a snack." I patted the space next to me on my bed. "Now sit down and have some chips with me."

Piper remained standing. "You never even let people drink water in your room. Aren't you worried there'll be oily crumbs all over your new comforter?"

I shrugged. "What are a few oily crumbs compared to the giant purple blob? Besides, I have to admit that it's kind of nice to stop worrying about my comforter."

"Well, if you're not going to worry, I certainly won't." Piper plopped down next to me and grabbed a big handful of chips.

"I missed talking to you so much," I said. "When I ate lunch with Rose and Jenna, they didn't get my jokes at all."

"I missed you too. When I ate with those girls from the band, they had a long, boring debate about who's the best clarinet player."

"*Ugh.* Rose and Jenna spent a very long time debating whether A. J. or Dominic is the cutest boy in school."

"That's ridiculous!" Piper said. "Obviously A. J. is the cutest."

I shook my head. "Dominic is way cuter than A. J. Haven't you seen Dominic's shiny, soulful eyes?"

"Haven't you seen A. J.'s dark and dreamy eyes?" Piper asked.

"Let's not get into a long, boring debate. They're both cute," I said, even though Dominic was definitely cuter than A. J.

"Yeah, let's not argue. We've done too much of that lately," Piper said.

We stayed on my bed awhile, snacking, listening to music, and joking around.

We'd just about finished the bag of chips when Eve came into my room. She wore a huge, hideous, hairy spider costume.

"Hey, Eve," Piper said. "You look cool."

If that was what cool looked like, I much preferred the uncool look.

"I just worked at the worst party ever," Eve said. "A couple of the little kids there screamed hysterically when they saw me. I don't blame them. And the birthday boy's dog chewed off one of my spider legs. There has to be an easier way to earn money."

"I agree. Now please leave so I can do homework," I said. I actually wanted her to leave so I wouldn't have nightmares about big arachnoids.

After Eve walked away, I asked Piper, "Do you want to work on our homework together? The English class essay is due tomorrow."

Piper wrinkled her nose. "I'm allergic to homework. I'm going home to watch TV and surf the Net."

Her parents were never going to let her have her phone back.

After Piper left, I hugged my phone and vowed to keep it with me always. Then I checked it for messages, on the off chance I had any.

I did have messages—eight of them! The first was from Mrs. Doyle, begging me to come back and babysit. I deleted it. The next message was also from Mrs. Doyle, begging me even harder. Deleted.

The third message was from someone who'd gotten my flyer. She wanted a sitter for her six-year-old boy, who she said was well-behaved and had an early bedtime. Yes!

The fourth message came from another neighbor who'd gotten my flyer. She had nine-year-old twin girls who she said were very easy. Double yes!

The fifth and sixth messages were also from Mrs. Doyle. She used the words *please* four times and *desperate* five times, but never used the words *raise your rate*, *pay you more*, or anything like that. Delete. Delete.

The next message said, "Hi, Kaitlyn. This is Harrison."

I sure hadn't expected a call from him. I wondered how he'd even gotten my phone number.

As if he'd read my mind, he said, "I got your number from that flyer you left at my house."

Oh.

"Just wanted to thank you for telling me about that easy babysitting job. I'm going to sit for the Doyles on Sunday night."

My stomach hurt. The bird was back and it was mad. It flapped its wings and pecked inside me. I tried to distract myself by listening to the last message on my phone. It was from my former client, Mrs. Sweet. "Hello, Kaitlyn," she said brightly. "I want to apologize for letting you go. That was a mistake. Doc didn't work out for us after all."

I smiled. Maybe it was evil to be happy about Doc's screwup. But maybe it wasn't. Doc had stolen my job, after all. Maybe it was karma.

"We'd like you to babysit again on Saturday nights," Mrs. Sweet said. "Please call me back. We miss you, Kaitlyn."

I missed them too. It wasn't just the money I missed. I missed Lucy's eager hugs and Mikey's mischievous smile and their parents' trust in me. I returned Mrs. Sweet's call.

"Kaitlyn! I'm so glad you called!" she gushed. "Can you babysit for Mikey and Lucy on Saturday nights again?"

"What happened with Doc?" I asked. It was none of my business, but I was dying to hear how he'd messed up.

"Well, I'm sure he meant well. And the children are very fond of him. But they got sick to their stomachs from all the junk food Doc gave them last Saturday. And he played tag with them in the house, breaking an expensive vase in the living room."

"I'm so sorry to hear that." I said, relieved that Mrs. Sweet couldn't see my big grin.

"So will you come back? Please?"

After she had been disloyal and fired me? Of course I'd come back. I loved Mikey and Lucy, and I needed the money. But I wasn't going to act like a doormat, letting Mrs. Sweet walk all over me. So I told her, "I've raised my rate a dollar an hour."

After a long pause, Mrs. Sweet said, "All right. We'll pay a dollar more an hour."

"Great. I'll see you Saturday." I hung up.

Then I returned the other calls and lined up two new babysitting jobs.

What a fantastic day I'd had! Well, apart from eating lunch with my annoying neighbors, feeling guilty about lying to Harrison, embarrassing myself in English class, and spending the afternoon in detention.

Sitter Smarts

Keeping children active
makes them happy and
burns off extra energy.

Chapter 8

I grinned when I saw Mikey and Lucy on Saturday night. "I'm so happy to be here! I missed you so much!" I said.

Mikey nodded as if he were just being polite.

After looking at her big brother, Lucy nodded politely too.

"We're glad to have our responsible sitter back," Mrs. Sweet said.

Mikey yawned.

Lucy copied him with a fake yawn.

My grin turned into a fake grin.

"We only hired Doc in the first place because we knew he needed the money," Mrs. Sweet said. "We used to eat at the restaurant his parents owned. It was a lovely place, but it never had many customers. Doc's parents were losing money on it and had to shut it down last month."

Suddenly I felt sorry for Doc. My parents didn't make a lot of money, but they both had jobs. Still, Doc shouldn't have let Mikey and Lucy eat so much junk food or play tag in the house. He'd gotten them sick and broken their parents' vase. And now they no longer seemed happy with a responsible sitter like me.

After Mr. and Mrs. Sweet left, I told the children, "I have a brand new babysitting bag." My dad had given me an old beige linen tote bag. Piper had drawn bright stars and happy faces on it and glued a large red ribbon on the top of it. I held up the bag.

Mikey glanced at the bag and shrugged.

Lucy copied him.

I kept my grin plastered on and said, "I brought the games you like and some great library books."

"Okay. I guess we can play a game." Mikey sighed, as if I'd just suggested a game of Clean Your Room or Do Your Homework.

"Or we can read a book." Lucy sighed, as if the books I'd brought were etiquette guides or math textbooks.

I dropped my grin and said, "We don't have to do those things. Do you have another idea?"

"Can you make cookies with us, like Doc did?" Mikey asked. "We had so much fun. Except we ate too much batter and got sick."

"Mommy said we can't do that anymore," Lucy said.

"So we can't make cookies," I said. That was a good thing. I had never baked cookies or anything else. If I tried, the cookies would probably turn out terrible. Or worse, I might ruin the Sweets' oven or burn down the kitchen.

"We can do another fun thing," I said. Unfortunately, I couldn't manage to think of another fun thing.

"Too bad we can't play octopus tag. That was *so* much fun—at least until we broke Mommy's vase," Lucy said.

"Doc told us that next time he came, he'd bring flashlights and glow-in-the-dark necklaces so we could play outside," Mikey said. "Did you bring any of that stuff?"

I shook my head.

Mikey sighed again. "I guess we'll have to play your memory game or read a book."

Lucy sighed again too. "I guess so."

"Maybe I can do something else Doc did with you," I said.

"He brought over a shoebox and cardboard and egg cartons. We made a dollhouse and little furniture," Lucy said.

That was actually a great idea. I was impressed. I sighed now. "I don't have a shoebox or cardboard or egg cartons with me."

"Doc also taught me a really funny dance," Lucy said.

"He showed me how to dribble a basketball, and he fixed my broken toy," Mikey added.

The kids seemed excited now that they were talking about Doc. He sounded amazing. I couldn't blame the kids for preferring him over me. And if Doc was Dominic, he was not only a fun babysitter, but a very cute one too. I said, "Is Doc a nickname for a longer name?"

Mikey nodded.

"Is it short for Dominic?"

"Huh?" Mikey said.

"I thought maybe Doc was short for Dominic, because they sound alike."

"No. Doc is the nickname of Julius Erving."

"Who?" I asked.

"Julius Erving. Doc said he's a famous old basketball player. Doc loves basketball."

So maybe Doc wasn't really Dominic after all. Then who was he? The mystery babysitter was into basketball. But that didn't narrow things down much. A lot of guys loved basketball.

"Doc showed us a really old Julius Erving basketball card," Mikey said. "Doc collects them."

Basketball card? That narrowed things down a lot. I knew someone who liked basketball cards.

"Julius Erving played for the 76ers," he added.

I knew a big 76ers fan too—the same guy who liked basketball cards. "Do you know what Doc's real name is?" I asked. Mikey nodded.

"What is it?"

"I told you. Julius Erving. The old basketball player." Mikey looked at me like I was an idiot.

I was an idiot. All this time I'd assumed that Doc was short for Dominic, but I'd obviously been wrong. And I'd been talking to the real Doc almost every day.

"I bet your other babysitter's real name is Harrison," I said.

"Yeah!" Mikey shouted happily. "Do you know him?"

I nodded.

"Can you tell him we miss him?" Lucy said.

"I will," I said. After I apologized to him. And to Dominic.

Then I realized something else: Harrison's parents had lost their restaurant business. Harrison needed this babysitting job a lot more than I did.

"Doc promised to show us how to fold paper into planes that could fly across the room and boats that could float in the bathtub," Mikey said.

Of course he did. He was Superbabysitter, able to leap tall buildings and entertain children in a single bound.

Well, if Harrison could do it, so could I. Maybe not in a single bound, but in two or three. "Doc sounds terrific," I said. "Maybe I can make airplanes and sailboats too."

"You know how?" Lucy asked.

"Not exactly," I said. "Actually, not at all. But I bet there's a YouTube video that can help."

There were lots of YouTube videos. We watched a few and tried to follow along. The planes didn't end up flying very well and the boats sank, but we all had fun.

The best part of the night was the water fight that broke out in the bathroom. I didn't try to stop it—because I had started it. We all dried the bathroom afterward, wiping up the water with old towels while singing "Rain, Rain, Go Away" at the top of our lungs.

Time flew, even though our airplanes did not. Before I knew it, it was Mikey and Lucy's bedtime. Our activities had tired them out, so getting them to sleep was a breeze. By the time Mr. and Mrs. Sweet arrived home, I'd filled out the parental checklist and done all my homework.

Mrs. Sweet paid my higher rate and added a generous tip. "I hope you can babysit for us every Saturday night," she said.

"I can come next Saturday night. But I can't promise I'll be free every week. I have other clients now," I said, trying not to sound too smug. "But Doc can babysit. Mikey and Lucy told me about him. They really miss him. If you give him another chance, I bet he'll work out great."

"I'll think about it," Mrs. Sweet said.

I'd been thinking about Doc AKA Harrison a lot tonight. I was happy to have my old job back, but I wished I could help Harrison earn money. And Piper too. If she had a job, she could buy more stuff for the pets she adored. I also wanted to help Eve earn enough money to leave her horrible job.

"Kaitlyn." Mrs. Sweet's voice startled me. "I asked you a question, but you seem lost in thought."

"Sorry. What is it?"

"Did you do something to the bathroom?"

Uh-oh. Time to fess up about our water fight. I took a deep breath.

"What did you use to clean the bathroom?"

"Um, water and towels mostly," I said in a shaky voice.

"It looks terrific. Thank you very much," Mrs. Sweet said.

I slowly exhaled and said, "You're welcome."

Sitter Smarts

Team up with another babysitter for increased efficiency and mutual support.

Chapter 9

The next morning, Mom took me to the discount store and showed me a dress she thought was "lovely." It was gray, high-collared, ankle-length, and deeply discounted. The dress would be perfect . . . if I wanted to repel boys. "Thanks, anyway," I told my mother. "But I'm going to buy a different dress with my babysitting money."

I left the clothing section of the discount store to search for supplies to add to my new babysitting bag. In the party aisle, I got balloons to blow up and toss around. In the crafts area, I picked out yarn and colored paper for the kids to glue onto lunch bags to make puppets. Finally, I got a children's joke book, using Piper's suggestion from a few weeks ago. I couldn't wait to share all these things with Mikey and Lucy and the other children I'd be babysitting.

First, though, I had to do something I'd been dreading all morning. After we left the discount store, I asked my mother to drop me off at Harrison's house.

His father answered the door. He was tall and kind of gangly like Harrison. He stared at me and asked, "Are you preaching your religion or looking for a lost pet?"

"Neither of those things," I replied.

"Good. I'm not looking to change religions, and I haven't seen any loose dogs or cats. If you're selling Girl Scout cookies, I'd like six boxes of Thin Mints."

I shook my head. "I'm here to see Harrison. My name is Kaitlyn Perez."

"Oh. Come on in, Kaitlyn."

"Um, no thank you." Harrison would soon be furious with me. I needed to stay outside in order to make a quick getaway.

"Harrison!" Mr. Knox called. "Kaitlyn Perez is here to see you."

Harrison came to the door quickly. "Hello, stalker," he teased.

"Hello, Doc," I said.

Harrison's eyes widened in surprise. He joined me on the front porch, gave his father a quick wave, and closed the front door behind him. "You found out?" he asked.

I nodded. "Mikey and Lucy Sweet helped me figure it out last night when I was at their house. They miss you a lot."

"I'm sorry, Kaitlyn."

"I'm sorry. For something else," I said. "I misled you about the Doyles. They have five children."

"That's all right. I can handle five children."

"That's what I had thought too. Until I got there." I shivered as I recalled the real-life nightmare of sitting for the Doyles. "There are two very whiny girls, twin boys who aren't potty-trained, and a baby who cries a lot. Plus, there's an awful pet mouse."

Harrison frowned at me. "You said the Doyles were easy."

"I totally lied. That's why I'm apologizing. The Doyles aren't merely difficult. They're impossible. Call up Mrs. Doyle and tell her you're too sick to babysit tonight," I said. "No, don't tell her that. She'll call you every day to ask when you'll be well enough to watch her children. Tell her you've moved away—far away, to another country, like Iceland or maybe to Antarctica. Or pretend that you're calling from prison, where you've just begun serving a life sentence with no parole."

"It can't be that bad," Harrison said. But he had turned pale.

"It's not that bad," I said. "It's worse."

Harrison sighed. "I need the money."

I reached into my jeans pocket and pulled out the money Mrs. Sweet had paid me the night before. "Take this. It'll help ease my guilt."

Harrison shook his head. "I'm not taking your hard-earned cash. You survived the Doyles, right?"

"Just barely."

"So they're not impossible like you just said. More like improbable."

"They're horrible!" I cried.

Harrison jutted his chin. "If you can survive them, so can I."

I'd never be able to convince him to stay away from the Doyles' house tonight. Instead, I'd have to make a huge sacrifice, much harder than offering Harrison my money. I took a deep breath and said, "If you promise not to accuse me of stalking you, I'll go to the Doyles' house with you tonight to help out."

"I promise." Harrison grinned. "Thanks a lot. I might be able to take care of the kids, but I definitely can't handle a rodent."

"My friend Piper can. I'll see if she can come along to help us. Believe it or not, she actually likes rodents. She even owned a rat as a pet," I said. We both shuddered.

As I walked back from Harrison's house, my relief about telling him the truth was over-shadowed by terror over what awaited us in a few hours.

When I got home, my mom said, "I can tell by looking at you that things didn't go well with Harrison."

"He insisted on sticking with his promise to babysit the Doyle children. So I offered to help him," I said.

Mom put her arm around me. "I'm proud of you, Mija. You did the right thing."

"I guess I did." Famous last words. "If I'm not home by midnight, assume the Doyle children have killed me. Is exhausting someone to death a crime?" I asked.

"Sounds like you may worry yourself to death before you even get there. All the energy you spend worrying can be put to much better use."

Mom took me to the food pantry she volunteered at. My mood lifted as soon as I got to work. I carefully separated the cake flour and whole-wheat flour from the all-purpose flour. I alphabetized cans of soup, arranged each type of spice by its expiration date, and organized many other items. At the end of the afternoon, the workers thanked me for my work, and I thanked them for helping me take my mind off the Doyles.

But my worries soon returned, and they grew stronger by the minute. I had to practically force myself into my dad's car that evening. As my dad drove Harrison, Piper, and me to the Doyles' house, I briefly considered flinging open the car door and making a run for it.

Harrison, sitting next to me, sniffed dramatically and said, "So that's what the scent of fear smells like."

"A few minutes with the Doyle kids and their mouse, and you'll smell like that too," I said.

I didn't bring my babysitting bag this time. I wanted to protect it from popsicle juice and other dangerous elements. Piper had a tote bag with her, though. I pointed to it and asked, "What's in there?"

"Things to do tonight," she said.

"Like coloring books and toys?" I asked.

"Things for me to do tonight. A couple of fashion magazines and a celebrity gossip magazine."

"Since you plan on reading, why not bring the book we're supposed to read for English class?" I asked.

She frowned. "Why would I want to do that?"

I shook my head.

We took our time getting out of my dad's car and walking to the Doyles' front door and the horror that lay behind it.

The door opened while we were still several yards away from it. Mrs. Doyle must have been lying in wait for us. "Three of you?" she said. "I'm paying only the one rate we agreed on."

We nodded. I heard children screaming in another room. I grabbed Piper's hand so she couldn't run away—and so I couldn't run away.

"I made hot dogs and peas for dinner. Check on the baby. He's in his crib," Mrs. Doyle said. Then she and Mr. Doyle ran out, yelling, "We're free!" and slamming the door shut behind them.

"I'm *huuuungry*," Madison whined.

"Me *tooooo*," Lauren whined.

One of the twins ran over, wiped his hand on Piper's pants leg, and said, "Booger."

Piper stepped back and made retching noises. "Bye. I'll be hiding out in the garage with my magazines for the rest of the night," she said.

"But what about the mouse? You told me you'd take care of it," I said.

"You." Piper pointed to Madison. "Show me where the mouse is. I'll bring it into the garage with me."

"But I'm *huuuungry*," Madison whined.

"Mouse first. Dinner second," Piper said.

Madison directed her to the mouse cage.

Piper turned and looked at me. "Kaitlyn, I'll let you know if there are any problems with the mouse. If there are any problems with these monstrous children, you're on your own."

The baby started wailing. I wailed on the inside.

"I'll get the baby," Harrison said.

"I'll feed the kids," I said.

I gave the children dinner while Harrison fed the baby a bottle, changed his diaper, and got him into pajamas.

The kids ate the hot dogs, but none of them would touch their peas. I didn't blame them. I couldn't stand peas. But I didn't tell the children that. Instead, I said, "Eat your peas. They'll help you grow big and strong."

"I don't even want to grow big and strong!" Madison said.

Lauren crossed her arms. "Peas look like great big boogers."

"And they taste like big boogers," one of the twins said.

"They're yucky-stinky," the other twin said.

Harrison walked over to the table, holding the baby in one arm. "I love peas," he said.

"You can have mine." Madison stood up.

"Stay at the table and eat your peas," I said firmly.

"No!" one of the twins said.

"No!" the other twin said.

"You're a mean old meanie!" Lauren said.

Madison sat down, scooped her peas under her plate, and looked up, saying, "There. My peas are all gone."

Harrison walked over to me and whispered, "Why don't we give the pea issue a rest? The kids won't die from skipping a veggie for one night."

Hmm. He had a point. I never ate peas and I was still alive. Besides, just babysitting the Doyles was hard enough. We couldn't be expected to act like food police too. So I said, "Never mind about the peas. They're causing too much trouble. Don't eat them."

"I like trouble. And you can't tell me what to do!" Lauren said. "I'm eating them."

"Me too!" Madison grabbed some of the peas from under her plate and popped them in her mouth.

I hid a smile. Madison and Lauren were so stubborn, they wanted to do whatever I didn't want them to do.

"Girls, do not eat the peas," Harrison said. He must have realized how stubborn they were too. "Peas are for boys—big strong boys."

"I'm a big strong boy," Evan or Ethan said.

"Me too," his twin said. They both ate their peas.

"Anything boys can do, girls can do better," Madison said.

"Yeah," Lauren said. The girls finished all their peas.

Harrison winked at me.

I winked back at him. Maybe the Doyles weren't so difficult after all.

Then Madison yelled, "I want a popsicle!"

"Me too!" Lauren yelled even louder.

The baby started crying in Harrison's arms.

The twins chanted, "We want popsicles, we want popsicles, we want popsicles."

The Doyles were so difficult after all.

"Popsicles are unhealthy. They're full of sugar," I said. "And they're messy and sticky and they stain things. Your popsicles ruined my new comforter."

All the children chanted, "We want popsicles, we want popsicles, we want popsicles."

I looked at Harrison for help. He was holding the crying baby while texting on his phone. "Harrison! Don't text on the job. Act like a professional and help me out here," I snapped.

"I am helping you," he said, still texting.

My phone dinged with a text message. I raised my eyebrows at Harrison, took my phone out of my pocket, and read Harrison's text: *Popsicles r sticky but u shouldn't be a stickler.*

I stared at my phone. It was hard to think around the chanting children and crying baby. But I realized one thing: Harrison's advice was good. Rules and healthy eating and tidiness were important, but sweet treats were okay sometimes. Mr. and Mrs. Doyle must have thought so too, since the popsicles were in their house. I needed to chill. And what was more chill than a frozen popsicle?

"All right, kids," I said, "you can all have popsicles—"

They stopped chanting and started cheering.

I held up my hand to stop them. "But first you need to clear the table. Bring your plates and forks into the kitchen and throw your dirty napkins in the trash," I said.

While they cleared their places and Harrison calmed the baby, I hurried into the garage to check on Piper—and to get a break.

Piper sat on the garage floor, cradling the mouse in her arms and singing "Somebody to Love." Yuck. I wasn't sure what made me queasier—that Piper was singing a Justin Bieber song or that she was singing it to a mouse.

"Do you want to eat popsicles with us in the kitchen?" I asked, keeping my distance from the rodent in Piper's arms.

"That depends," she said. "Will the ankle biters be there?"

"Huh?"

"Ankle biters. Rug rats. Snot monsters. The scourge of the Earth."

"Okay, I get it. We civilized people like to call them children," I said. "Of course they'll be there. We're babysitting them."

"Thanks, but I'll stay in the garage. I greatly prefer the company of the mouse," Piper said.

I rolled my eyes and returned to the house. The children were thrilled to get popsicles. Harrison and I were thrilled to get some peace.

Unfortunately, chaos soon resumed. We divided and conquered. I got one twin down from the kitchen counter while Harrison took the other one off the top of a dresser. While I made sure the girls brushed their teeth and changed into pajamas, Harrison gave the boys piggy-back rides. While I got the boys ready for bed, Harrison played Legos with the girls. I read the kids bedtime stories while Harrison rocked the baby to sleep.

After the children were asleep, Piper came out of the garage and quietly returned the caged mouse to the girls' bedroom. Then we all cleaned the house and collapsed on the living room sofa.

"There has to be an easier way to earn money," Harrison said with a sigh.

"And a more profitable way," I said. "I have an idea."

"Spill it, Kaitlyn," Piper said.

"Not yet. I'm still working everything out in my head."

"Once you make your fortune, can I have the babysitting jobs you don't have time for?" Harrison asked.

"Sure. But you might be too busy making a fortune with me. You and Piper and my sister."

"As long as it doesn't involve the Doyles or mice, I'm in," he said.

I grinned at him. I really hoped I could make my idea work.

Sitter Smarts

Babysitters must
be punctual.

Chapter 10

On Monday, I looked for Dominic before school and during lunchtime, but I didn't see him. So I got to English class early and stood by the door. Unfortunately, Dominic didn't show up until right before the bell rang.

I sat at my desk and tried to pay attention to Ms. Roach. "Passive language will be discussed by me during today's class," she said. "Writing is made unnecessarily tedious by the application of passive language."

Harrison raised his hand. "Are you using passive language on purpose to show us how tedious it sounds?"

Ms. Roach frowned. "No. There was no intent to make use of passive language."

"There you go again," Harrison said.

The class laughed.

Ms. Roach glared at Harrison before droning on once more.

My mind drifted to the business venture I was planning and then to the apology I owed Dominic. I sneaked a look at him. He was staring at me.

I didn't know why Dominic had stared at me before, but I was pretty sure he did it today because he was angry that I'd yelled at him.

I caught his eye. He really did have nice eyes. He was very cute.

I looked at Ms. Roach again.

"Passive language should not be used by writers," she said. "Markdowns will be given by me when passive language is apparent in your essays."

When the bell finally rang, I rushed out of the room and stood on the other side of the door. As soon as Dominic exited, I said, "Can I talk to you?"

He blushed. "Me?"

"Yes." I felt myself blushing too. "Please."

We walked a few feet down the hallway, avoiding the mob of kids streaming from the classrooms. Then I stopped and said, "I'm sorry for yelling at you last week. I was really rude."

Dominic gave a little shrug. "I'm sorry you got in trouble for it." There were a few seconds of awkward silence. Then he added, "And I'm sorry for staring at you."

I gave a little shrug. Hearing him acting so nice made me feel even guiltier. I never should have assumed he was Doc. And I shouldn't have assumed the real Doc—Harrison—was a bad guy.

There were a few more seconds of awkward silence.

Finally, Dominic said, "I can't help staring at you, because . . ." He trailed off and blushed even more. Then he took a deep breath and talked really fast. "Because I think you're pretty and smart and are you going to the eighth-grade dance?"

Wow. Wow, wow, wow. I blushed even more.

"Yes, she's going," Piper said. She was standing next to me, which I hadn't even noticed. "And, Dominic, wait until you see Kaitlyn's new dress," Piper added. "You may not think it's possible, but the dress makes her look even more beautiful than she already is. Are you going to the dance, Dominic?"

He nodded. And nodded. And nodded.

"You and Kaitlyn had better dance together," Piper said.

I nodded and nodded and nodded.

"We're going to be late to our classes," Piper said. "I'm always late. It doesn't bother me at all. But for some strange reason, you two seem to care about tardies and grades and stuff like that."

"Oh! Bye." I hurried away.

"Bye, Kaitlyn! Save a dance for me," Dominic called out. His voice was very shaky.

It was the best sound I'd ever heard.

Sitter Smarts

Babysitters who are
in demand can charge
more money.

Chapter 11

Lucy jumped up and down with excitement as her first guest walked toward the park.

My stomach jumped up and down with nerves. This was my first time organizing a children's party. I reminded myself that I was well prepared. I'd reserved the picnic area of the park, sent out the invitations, and scheduled the day's events. Even better, I had a lot of help.

I took a deep breath. Then I walked with Lucy and her family to greet Lucy's guest. I smiled at the little girl, who said her name was Julia, and shook her father's hand.

"Hello, I'm Kaitlyn Perez, the head of KPHE Super Fun Party Services," I said. "Parents are welcome to stay at Lucy's party, or you may drop off your daughter. Just be sure to return by three o'clock."

I handed the man a business card printed with the name of our business, my cell phone number, and www.KPHEparties.com, the website Eve had made for us. In the center of the card Piper had sketched an adorable picture of happy children around a birthday cake. The back of the card was blank. I'd nixed Piper's suggestion to write: "We'll do all the work while you sit around on your lazy behinds."

"Julia, I'm happy to bring your present to the gift table, or you can take it there yourself," I told the little girl in front of me. I pointed to a picnic table covered with a tablecloth Piper had decorated with pictures of cute balloons. I added, "Do you see the pretty princess at the table? That's Princess Eve. She's the best face-painter in the entire kingdom."

I had let Lucy pick Eve's costume, but I'd limited her choices to princess, yoga girl, or clown.

Eve thought the costumes were a zillion times better than the sunflower, chicken, and other monstrosities she had to wear at her former job. She had hoped Lucy would choose yoga girl, so she could wear a comfy T-shirt and yoga pants. But the princess costume wasn't bad.

Eve wore a long gown we'd found at a thrift shop, accessorized with a tiara and pink ballet flats from the discount store. And it was better than dressing up as a clown, which meant wearing the ugly green and orange striped dress our mom had wanted to buy me for the eighth-grade dance.

"Princess Eve will be here for the entire party. So will Doc," I said. I pointed to Harrison, who stood by the playground. "He knows lots of great games, cool races, and funny jokes."

"He's super fun! He babysits me and my brother sometimes," Lucy said.

I nodded. I still loved sitting for them every Saturday night, but Mr. and Mrs. Sweet had gone out for Sunday brunch the last two weeks while Harrison watched the kids.

"Also, Piper and Pets will be coming," I said.

"Piper is Kaitlyn's friend," Mrs. Sweet explained. "She's going to show us her animals."

"She's bringing her snake!" I said, trying to sound happy instead of horrified.

"A snake?" Julia's father frowned. He was obviously with me on Team Horrified.

"Piper's snake is very sweet and tame," I said, trying not to shiver. "Piper's also bringing her bearded dragon lizard. He's adorable." More awful than adorable, but that was just my opinion.

I handed Julia her name tag, which Piper had decorated with flowers and butterflies.

"Kaitlyn, is there anything at all I can do?" Mrs. Sweet asked.

"Yes." I smiled. "You can relax and have fun and leave everything to Eve, Piper, Harrison, and me."

I spotted another child, wide-eyed and biting his lower lip, walking slowly to the park while clutching his mother's hand. I excused myself and made my way toward him. I moved slowly, as I'd first done for Aiden, the six-year-old I now babysat on Friday nights. Aiden had been timid at first, but now when he saw me he was all hugs, laughter, and chatter.

I met the boy at the entrance to the park, crouched down, and said, "Hi. I'm Kaitlyn. Are you here for Lucy's party?"

His mother nodded. "We sure are. This is Jonah. He's a little shy."

"I'm a little shy too," I said. Then I pointed out Princess Eve, sitting by herself at the picnic table. "It's nice and quiet over there." I offered to walk him over. Jonah could start there and get comfortable before heading toward Harrison, who was calling for Lucy's friends to join his games.

Lucy's guests trickled into the party. Eve painted their faces, Harrison played games with them, and I watched them enjoy the playground equipment. We all took lots of pictures.

The party was going strong when Piper arrived, lugging her snake and lizard cages. I rushed over and asked, "Piper, are you sure those cages are secure? You say your snake is harmless, but if Sweetcakes gets out, I'll die from fright. Who knows what the kids will do!"

Piper rolled her eyes. "The cages are secure. There's nothing to be afraid of."

Of course not. Why would anyone be afraid of cold-blooded, scaly creatures with long, fierce, forked, fast-moving tongues?

After Piper set the cages on a picnic bench, she asked, "Have you come back to Earth yet after the dance last night?"

I smiled. "My feet are back on the ground, but my heart is still soaring high." Piper pretended to throw up. We both laughed.

"You and Dominic really looked gorgeous together. You two danced so much!" Piper said.

"I felt gorgeous in my new dress. What an awesome night! And congratulations again for winning the dance contest," I said. Piper had done the Overly Caffeinated Lobster, the Confused Kangaroo, and other hilarious dances she'd made up.

"Kaitlyn!" Harrison yelled. "Come here and compete in the Goofypalooza race!"

"Is Goofypalooza appropriate for someone of my stature? After all, I'm the head of a successful company," I said to Piper.

"Get out there!" She gave me a little push toward Harrison.

I hurried over to compete in the race. First, we had to hop on one foot while singing "Mary Had a Little Lamb." Then we had to hit Harrison with a water balloon. Finally, we hopped backward, rang a bell, and yelled "Goofypalooza!" The race was ridiculous. And I enjoyed every minute of it. I hadn't had so much fun since . . . well, since the night before at the dance.

"Now it's time for the Piper and Pets show! Follow me," I announced. I led the kids to Piper and her awful animals.

When she saw us coming, Piper frowned and said, "Don't sit too close. I'm allergic to children."

Piper didn't like children, but they loved her and her pets. Even I—an avowed reptile detester—thought Piper put on a great show. She showed the kids Sweetcakes and told them about all kinds of snakes. She said that flying snakes jump from tree to tree, black mamba snakes slither faster than most athletes can run, and boy garter snakes have to fight for a girlfriend snake, since there are 10,000 males for every female.

Then Piper took her bearded dragon lizard, Snookums, out of his cage. As she snuggled with him, she said Snookums loved to eat crickets, locusts, and worms. I tried not to gag. Piper taught the children about bearded dragon lizards. Sometimes they changed colors when they were scared. Thirty years ago, there weren't any bearded dragon lizards in America. "The good old days," I muttered. Finally, Piper let the kids pet Sweetcakes and Snookums and answered questions.

After the Piper and Pets show, we sang "Happy Birthday" to Lucy and served the cake. Lucy had asked for a chocolate cake. She sure got it. Harrison had made a huge chocolate cake with chocolate fudge filling and chocolate icing, topped with chocolate chips and chocolate sprinkles.

The children gobbled it up. "This is the best-est party ever!" Lucy said. The other kids agreed, arguing only about what was the "funnest" part of the party: the cute "dragon beard lizard," "that crazy Doc guy," the "nice face-painter lady," or the most delicious cake in the "whole wild world."

I couldn't stop smiling. All our efforts had paid off. They would literally pay off once Eve, Piper, Harrison, and I split the huge check from Mr. and Mrs. Sweet. And many of the children had said they wanted us to run their parties and babysit for them. Both of these jobs made me very happy. KPHE Super Fun Party Services was already booked next Saturday afternoon, though it wasn't a paying gig. We'd be putting on a children's party at the homeless shelter.

After the kids finished eating, we quickly cleaned the picnic table and watched Lucy open her birthday presents.

Eve cut a small sliver of cake, put it on a paper plate, and grabbed a fork.

"That's so wrong," I told her.

Eve set down her fork. "I know you think it's wrong to eat a client's cake during her party. But it looks so delicious, it's hard to resist."

"No," I said. "It's wrong to take such a small piece of that amazing-looking cake after we all worked so hard today."

I cut myself a large slice and shoved a forkful in my mouth. I meant to say "delicious," but my mouth was so full it came out sounding like "Delihuh."

After I finished swallowing, I said, "If eating chocolate cake at the end of a successful event with your sister and your friends is wrong, then I don't want to be right."

"This party really is a success," Eve said. "I earned a lot more money today than I did at my old job."

I nodded. But success wasn't just about money. It was also about having a great time with my sister, my best friend, and my new friend, putting on an awesome party for adorable kids. Not to mention competing in Harrison's Goofypalooza race without falling and watching Piper handle her snake without screaming.

I grinned while Harrison and Piper cut slices for themselves. Then I shoved more cake in my mouth.

About the Author

A former lawyer, D. L. Green now writes books for children and teens. She lives in southern California with her family, including a silly dog named Edna. In addition to writing, D. L. enjoys reading, hiking, and horseback riding. She also loves giving writing workshops and talks at schools, libraries, and conferences for students, teachers, and writers.

Want more of The Babysitter Chronicles?
Check out this sneak peek of

Olivia Bitter, Spooked-Out Sitter

"It was a dark and stormy night," I said.

A gust of wind answered, sending a flutter of dead leaves skittering across the sidewalk. I shivered, took a deep breath, and turned the corner. The House loomed ahead. Dark windows, like evil eyes, glared down at me. Gnarled vines clawed the walls like fingers.

"It was a dark and stormy night." I said again, more softly this time. No one answered. I was alone. "A dark and stormy night" was how my longtime best friend, Beth, and I always started our ghost stories. Whenever we walked past The House (emphasis on each word: *The. House.*), we whispered stories we'd imagined about the ghosts and murderers and creatures and villains who lived within its walls. My stories were scary, but Beth's usually made us giggle, which helped ease our fears when walking past *The. House.*

But today I was alone. Just like every day this week . . . and last week . . . and the week before. Ever since we'd started seventh grade a few months ago, Beth had made up one excuse after another to avoid walking home from school with me.

She'd say, "I'm going to stay after to make posters for Spirit Week," or, "My mom is picking me up and we're going to the mall," or, "I'm going to help Mr. Billings clean up the science room."

All excuses, never the truth.

The truth was that Beth was becoming Miss Popular, and I was anything but. She didn't want to be seen with me anymore. She preferred to spend her time with the cool crowd, especially her new best friend, Avery.

Beth and I had been best friends all through elementary school. When we started junior high, I didn't think anything would change—not about our friendship, anyway. That first day, hundreds of new faces lined the halls and cafeteria, and Beth and I stuck close together. But after that first day, things did change. Beth changed. She wasn't interested in anything we used to do, like watching anime cartoons or making up ghost stories. Now she was only interested in the latest fashions and designer boots.

Beth was really focused on what everyone else was wearing too. She and Avery took turns carrying around a secret notebook. Inside, they wrote down everything all the girls in our class wore every day. Next to each girl's name, they'd draw a smiley face for clothes they liked or a frowny face for clothes they didn't.

How did I know this? Well, one day last week, when Beth reluctantly agreed to come over after school, I peeked at the notebook while she was in the bathroom. Of course, I looked for my name. Frowny faces for every single day. And Beth had even written "Yuck!" next to my manga T-shirt. I was stunned. Beth had always liked that shirt. At least, she'd always said she did.

What upset me the most is Beth knew how much I loved manga comics. She knew my dream was to write my own manga-style series one day. I knew Beth didn't love manga as much as I did (probably no one did), but the fact that she would make fun of it devastated me.

After she left that day, I told my mom I needed new clothes. My mom laughed. "We just bought you a bunch of new clothes for school," she said.

Yeah, a couple new manga T-shirts and a Wonder Woman sweater. I knew I'd get more "Yucks" next to my name if I wore those. "They're not the right clothes," I muttered.

"But you begged for them at the store!" Mom said, frowning in surprise.

I gave her my most convincing stare. "I would like a designer handbag. And suede boots. And a black skater skirt from Nordstrom," I told her. "Like the one Avery wore today."

Mom laughed. "The only way you're getting those is if you buy them yourself."

Myself? How on earth would I ever save up enough money?

Another gust of wind jolted me from my thoughts. I was nearing the block of *The. House.* Even though Beth and I had made up our stories about it, we knew it was definitely haunted. It had been abandoned forever—a crumbly old mansion with turrets and broken windows, an overgrown yard crawling with thorny weeds, and a tall, wrought-iron fence with sharp spires that would poke you you-know-where if you tried to climb over. I wouldn't be surprised if there was even a cemetery in the backyard. No one has lived there for years. *No one could live there,* I heard Beth's voice say in my head. *No one alive, that is. Only ghosts.* And for a split second, I thought I heard her cackling laughter.

And the strangest of them all is the spirit of a little girl, Lillian, I added. Lillian was my favorite ghost. *On a dark and stormy night, Lillian fell down the cellar steps, into a narrow hole. She cried for help, but no one could reach her. She wailed and wailed, and even after she died down there, she kept wailing . . .*

Sometimes her face appears at the window, Beth's voice continued. *And instead of just Boo! she yells, "Bibbledy-bobbledy-boo!"*

I started to laugh, but then I froze. A face appeared at the turret window.

And looked right at me.

And then vanished.

I let out a bloodcurdling scream and started to run. But then something, or someone, grabbed onto me.

I whirled to see a little girl holding on tightly to my jacket. Her skin was so pale I felt I could almost see through it. White-blond, ghostly hair wafted about her head. She stared at me without blinking even once.

Lillian. Lillian the cellar-ghost, right before my eyes.

I tugged my jacket, but she held fast. She let out a strange giggle.

"Let go!" I pleaded.

She shook her head solemnly. "Hi," she whispered. "Do you want to play?"

My heart raced. I closed my eyes. "No, please, no!" I moaned.

The front gate swung open with a clang. I opened my eyes and screamed again. In front of me stood a tall man with wild eyes and messy hair. His face was smeared with dirt. He looked like he'd just crawled from a grave.

"Please don't hurt me," I begged. "I'll do whatever you ask. Just please, don't—"

The man's loud laugh interrupted me. "Hurt you? Why would I hurt you?" he said. "I'm just a friendly neighbor."

"That's what they all say," I muttered. "To lure you in. And then . . ."

"You have quite the imagination!" the man said. He held out a grimy hand for me to shake. I just stared at it.

"Tell Lillian to let go of me," I said. "Please tell her to let go."

"Who's Lillian? This is my daughter Frannie. And I'm Bob Wolf. We just moved in."

"Wolf? Like the animal that bites? And howls at the moon?" I said.

Bob Wolf laughed. "Yes. The Wolfs!" Then he arched his neck and howled, like a wolf would. Lillian/Frannie giggled and howled too.

"Do you want to play?" Lillian/Frannie whispered again, after she'd stopped howling.

Mr. Wolf smiled. "She must like you!" he said to me. "She's usually shy around strangers."

My heart had stopped racing (for the time being). "You just moved in here?" I asked, nodding toward *The. House.*

Mr. Wolf sighed. "Yes. It's quite the fixer-upper." He shrugged. "But it has a fascinating history. Did you know that—"

"Bob?" a woman's voice called. I looked up to see the face at the turret window. A woman's face. A human face, not a ghost.

"Ah, Mommy's calling us!" Mr. Wolf said to Frannie. He turned to me. "But before we go, what is your name? You never told me."

I hesitated. I still felt a bit wary. "Olivia," I finally said. "Olivia Bitter."

Mr. Wolf raised his eyebrows. "Oh! I believe I met your mother today. She brought over some cookies as a housewarming gift."

"*Mmmm*, good!" Frannie said.

I nodded. "Mom's cookies are to die for," I said, instantly regretting my choice of words. "I mean, they're really good."

"Like I said," Mr. Wolf went on, "Frannie doesn't usually take to strangers. But she likes you, and we're in need of a babysitter next weekend . . ."

To find out what happens, pick up

Olivia Bitter, Spooked-Out Sitter

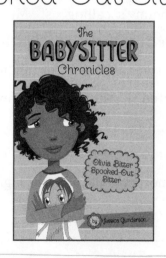